I0581089

Airship Daedalus

The Golden City

By Todd Downing

FIRST EDITION

ISBN: 978-1-7349293-9-3

Copyright © 2018 Todd Downing & Deep7 Press

All Rights Reserved Worldwide

Edited by Andrea Edelman

Additional editing by Dan Heinrich & Raechelle Downing

Cover art & design by Todd Downing
(*Daedalus* model by Hans Piwenitzky)

Based on the *Airship Daedalus / AEGIS Tales* setting and characters by Todd Downing and published in various media by Deep7 Press. *Airship Daedalus™* and *AEGIS Tales™* are trademarks of Deep7 Press.

WWW.AIRSHIPDAEDALUS.COM

Deep7 Press is a subsidiary of Despot Media, LLC
1214 Woods Rd SE Port Orchard, WA 98366 USA
WWW.DEEP7.COM

To my wife Raechelle
and my daughter Kayleigh,
My muses, my loves.

- PRELUDE -

Romania, March 1927

The echo of the officer's boots on the tile floor of the fortress on Straja Hill sounded like a unit of cavalry on parade. A strapping Dutch-German with cropped dark hair slicked back with nary a lock out of place, his thin mustache rested atop the chiseled line of a mouth. Gray eyes peered from below a sharp brow, and an officer's cap with crimson piping was tucked neatly under his arm. His black captain's uniform was neatly pressed, and displayed commendations from previous Silver Star operations. All save the last one. Project Liftoff had been a bust, thanks to the interference of a young AEGIS field agent, and Captain Ernst Hummel wanted vengeance.

He did not allow himself even the briefest view from the windows which looked out over Brasov and the surrounding Carpathian mountains. He knew this region from earlier naval service in the Black Sea during the war, and he didn't find it quaint or romantic. Others saw a cosmopolitan area where Slavs, Germans and Romani, Christians and Jews alike lived and worked together in relative harmony. Hummel saw a cesspool of cultural and moral weakness.

The doors to the great hall were already open, and the gray-clad commandos standing guard made no move to stop him, so Captain Hummel, the infamous *Schwarzhund* of the Silver Star, strode in directly, chin high and chest forward.

Crowley sat at the far end of a long banquet table. It was strewn with maps of different regions of the world, but presently he was distracted by a young Romanian woman feeding him bites of glazed pears seasoned with sugar and cloves. Now fifty-two, if Crowley had been out of shape just two years previous, he now bordered on obese. Dogged by ill health and a persistent heroin addiction, his hair had long ago surrendered—and while he was usually content to shave his head completely, he'd let it go these past months, leaving a pale dome surrounded by a short-clipped fringe of salt and pepper. His brown eyes looked at

Hummel from a bed of dark bags, his once-strong jaw now soft and jowly.

"Ah," Crowley said, halting his concubine's ministrations with the wave of a hand. "If it isn't the Black Dog himself!" His tone was snide, the words spoken in a proper English accent.

Captain Hummel snapped to attention at the opposite end of the table. "Master."

"Come closer," Crowley instructed, sending the woman away with a dismissive slap on the butt. Hummel frowned at the display or corrupt power, but said nothing. His situation was bad enough without challenging the sexist attitudes of the Great Beast of Mankind.

Hummel watched the Romanian woman exit the hall through a door to the interior as he approached the head of the table. He was braced to receive punishment for his failure in Shanghai, but his bearing was stoic and betrayed not an ounce of fear.

"Explain to me, Captain Hummel," Crowley sneered, "how a nearly operational Lenzium refinery, which should have been well beyond the reach of AEGIS saboteurs, goes up in flames." Crowley stood, almost matching Hummel's six feet in height, yet looming much larger in force of personality. "Through the actions of a single field agent, no less."

Hummel withstood the dressing-down without emotion. "I can offer no explanation," he said, "other than the operation itself and our countermeasures to the AEGIS infiltration were performed to Astrum Argentum rules of engagement." He stared into the brown eyes of his master, trying desperately to give the illusion of strength. "We simply did the best we could with the resources we had, and were caught lacking."

Crowley laughed aloud. "*Caught lacking??*" Suddenly his smile dropped as quickly as it had come and his face grew red with anger. "Our refinery was *destroyed!* Our anti-gravity prototype *stolen!*"

"Yes, sir," Hummel agreed. "All of which could have been avoided with the allocation of a few more covert agents in the city, and a single additional unit of commandos on the ground."

Crowley paused, letting the room go awkwardly silent. He turned away from Hummel and began to pace the floor behind the great wooden armchair at the head of the table. The silent pacing continued for an agonizing minute, Hummel beginning to sweat.

He hoped Crowley would believe his aggressiveness was genuine.

Finally, Crowley turned, looking him over appraisingly. "Captain Hummel," he addressed formally. "I hereby suspend your commission as commander of the destroyer *Silver Shark.*"

Here it comes, Hummel thought. *He's going to assign me to some backwater observation post where I shall die of malaria.* He wondered briefly about the recent discovery of mineral wealth in a remote valley in the Congo —perhaps Crowley would assign him there?

"Instead, I have a different position for you," Crowley added. "A post at which I think you will have every opportunity to succeed."

Hummel braced himself as Crowley ambled nearer.

"I am leaving for Tunisia tomorrow, and I need to be sure you will have this assignment well in hand."

Hummel snapped his heels together. "Yes, sir. Set any challenge, allow me to prove my loyalty and worth to the Astrum Argentum."

"Strong words," Crowley mocked. "Do not pose for my benefit, Captain. I see through your bravado and bluster. But the fact that you came here ready and willing to face punishment for your failure, and mustered enough courage to *try* and stare me down is *something*... and I think it would be shortsighted indeed if I executed every commander who failed an operation." The Master turned and flopped back down in his chair, musing. "No, I need commanders like you, Hummel. Provided you are the kind of man who learns from his mistakes."

"I am indeed, sir." Hummel remained at attention.

"Very well," said Crowley, signing a small form on the stack of maps and sealing it with red wax. "Your new commission, Captain Hummel."

The Black Dog bowed formally and accepted the paper from Crowley, who waved him away. Hummel didn't stay to read the commission; he marched crisply from the great hall, wanting to put as much distance between himself and Aleister Crowley as possible before the man changed his mind.

- CHAPTER 1 -

Scotland, April, 1927

A cruel wind whipped in from the North Atlantic. It smelled of salt and diesel, of dead fish and purple heather, with the occasional hint of peat smoke. It was a bitter, wet wind, scratching at anything in its path with a million icy talons. The ink-colored sea carried no shipping traffic, for the currents among the straits and eddies of the southern Hebrides were known to tear the sturdiest ships asunder on the most pleasant of days. The beneficent presence of an almost-full moon was lost on the barren, rocky ground, thanks to the blanket of blistering Atlantic weather above.

Dr. Dorothy Starr hugged her leather flight jacket close against the freezing winds and directed the beam of the field flashlight along the craggy trail. Her light criss crossed with Jack's as they continued on the path laid out on the centuries-old calfskin map they'd procured in Morocco from one of Louis' most trusted fences—or rather, "antiquities dealers". A slender brunette with sparkling green eyes and bee-stung bow lips, Starr—known by the unoriginal yet descriptive moniker "Doc"—was a dead ringer for Myrna Loy, the young actress who'd just been cast to play her in the serialized movie versions of the *Daedalus* adventures.

The isle of Scarba lay just off the west coast of Oban, a tiny mole on the neck of Jura, to the south. Separated from its larger southern cousin by the Gulf of Corryvreckan and its treacherous whirlpool, it was a land removed from time. Taking its name from the Old Norse for "sharp, stony, hilly terrain", Scarba was as advertised—"what's on the tin", as their colleague Edward "Duke" Willis used to say. Devoid of timber and any permanent dwellings, save a small fishing village on the eastern coast and a stone hunting lodge used seasonally by Arthur Hill, 6th Baron of Sandys, it was to the uneducated observer simply a dreary, brush-covered rock off the Scottish coast.

Doc was not an uneducated observer. She knew this island to be so much more than a place to graze sheep or hunt deer. She knew it to be a place where 14th century monks from Iona had built a complex beehive of cells as a retreat from warfare or plague. She also knew it to have been a place of strategic importance to the Picts of the Dark Ages, part of the Gaelic overkingdom of *Dál Riata*, a hallowed burial site for some of the most elite chieftains. And it was precisely one of those ancient Celtic crypts she and Jack were looking for, currently without much luck.

Jack McGraw blinked as the wind whipped around his head and upper body. He was a strapping man in his early thirties with a jaw that seemed chiseled from rose marble. It was that jaw—bristling with two day's worth of beard—a pair of piercing blue eyes, and a rakish half smile that made ladies everywhere swoon. Although rising star Gary Cooper had signed to play him in the flickers, Jack arguably got more attention than the actor when the two had gone out on the town together.

Jack shivered. The leather flight helmet did almost nothing to warm his ears, although it did help cut the wind noise. He kept the goggles in their raised position on his forehead. Blinking away the cold rain and mist was far easier than trying to clean the goggles every thirty seconds. But even with his own flashlight, it was impossible to see anything here. He pulled Doc aside to get a clear line of communication. "We've been combing this area for hours, Doc. Could this map be a phony?"

Doc got the gist of his point. Leaning close, she answered, "Louis obtained it from a reputable dealer. The entrance just has to be here. Somewhere."

As Jack ducked his gaze away from a buffet of wind, he noticed something to the side of the trail. An unusually straight line ran north-south between two sections of flat stone covered in moist green moss and purple heather. He traced the line with his flashlight, nudging his partner as he went. "Say, Doc," Jack indicated with a nod. "Shine your flashlight over here."

Doc turned and followed the beam from Jack's light with her eyes. "Sure," she said. "What do you see?"

Jack moved toward the granite blocks and ran a finger down the groove between them. "Right here, under these scrub plants? Looks like a seam in the rock."

Doc knelt next to him, and nodded. The unnaturally straight line was proximate to the where the map said the tomb entry was. She triangulated between their current location, the ancient path they'd come from, and a small circle of standing stones just a few paces west. It was the most promising lead they'd had. Reaching behind her head to her canvas backpack, she produced a three-foot-long steel pry bar, and handed it to Jack. "Go to it," she smiled.

"Thanks," came Jack's reply, but the intended sarcasm was lost to the whistling wind. He traded his flashlight to Doc and took a deep breath. Grasping the bar in his gloved hands, Jack planted the straight end in the seam between the stones and leaned forward with his entire weight. The bar fought him at first, with no movement below. Then, gradually, he felt a heavy scraping, and the seam widened as the stone on the east side of the line scooted several inches forward.

Doc leaned down and peered through the open slot with one of the lights. Not much was visible in the chamber below, save for a stone stairway that disappeared into the darkness.

This was it. It had to be.

Jack re-positioned the pry bar and leaned over again, but the flat end now had nothing to push against. The stone slab was a good three feet square, and five inches thick. Jack cleared away some moss and found the back edge of the slab, planting his boot to brace it. Then he hooked the curved end of the bar over the edge of the rock and hauled backward with his weight. This time, Doc grabbed hold of the open lip with her free hand and pulled along with him. After several moments of straining against the dead weight of ancient stone, the slab finally came up, toppling over backward. Jack whipped his foot away before the stone landed with a soft *thud* in the heather.

There before them lay the portal to an underground burial chamber, undisturbed for ten centuries, incognito beneath the uncaring wind.

Doc returned Jack's flashlight and let her own beam roam around beneath the opening. "Well, well, well," she muttered.

Jack nodded in agreement. "And a stairway leading down."

"But of course," Doc chimed, green eyes sparkling in the falloff from the flashlights. "You don't think I'd take you to one of those sleazy tombs without a stairway, do you?"

Jack hooked his flashlight to a ring on his belt. "You sure do know how to show a fella a good time."

"Sweet talker." Doc winked at him, returning the pry bar to her backpack with a single, samurai-like motion.

Jack pulled his pack from his shoulders and opened it to produce a box made of maple wood with tension clasps keeping two halves together. He set it on the edge of the step as Doc descended the first few stairs, exploring the walls with her flashlight.

Snapping open the clasps, Jack opened the hinged box to reveal a standard-issue two-way field radio. It featured a hand-cranked dynamo and a ten-mile range, although probably not half that tonight, not in this weather. Jack cranked the dynamo and plucked the handset from the cradle, setting the tuner to the predetermined frequency.

"Away party to *Daedalus*," he said. "Away party to *Daedalus*. Have located tomb. Estimate pickup in twenty."

There was a quiet electronic whine, a burst of static, then a woman's voice, tinged with a British accent, wafted from the speaker. "Affirmative, Captain Stratosphere. *Daedalus* standing by."

Jack rolled his eyes. "Rivets must've put her up to it," he moaned.

"They only do it because you react," Doc laughed.

"I've never even been to the stratosphere," he complained. "I got the call sign during the war, as a joke..."

It was Doc's turn to roll her eyes. "Yes. We know. Come on, Captain Stratosphere."

Jack closed up the radio and slung his pack onto his shoulders as he stepped down into the dim passageway.

"Ladies first," Doc said, edging a boot toward the next step down. "You back me up."

When Jack didn't answer, Doc turned to find him checking a nickel-plated .45 Colt automatic, slapping in a magazine and ratcheting back the slide. He actually kept a pair of them—something to do with a pilot's need for redundant systems—but apparently this Celtic warlord's crypt only warranted the one.

"Jack," Doc squinted at him through the wind. "This tomb has been sealed for at least a thousand years. What are you gonna do with that .45?"

"Doc," he answered, tone for tone. "Might I remind you that we've dealt with alligators, pirates, tree-dwelling Amazon natives, a giant octopus, rocket-zombies, and a secret mystical society whose agents dissolve into thin air when you catch them? I'm not taking any chances."

He was serious, and when he put it in those terms, she could find no fault in his logic. "Fair enough," she said. "Follow me."

She set her left foot on the hand-hewn stone and directed her flashlight beam into the void below. Jack followed three steps behind, pistol in his right hand, retrieving the flashlight from his belt-hook with his left.

They descended into the cold, ancient dark.

Jack and Doc stepped in silent, dance-like harmony. This was a couple who knew each other's habits and movements, and who knew danger intimately. The Great War had brought them together a decade ago. They'd been comrades in arms, lovers for a brief time, then strangers. Doc had married, borne a child, and become a widow within a few short years. Jack had gone into commercial aviation as a test pilot and mail courier. She'd come back into his life as an envoy for Thomas Edison's AEGIS organization, to draft him into service as the pilot of an experimental airship and leader of its crew. Together they'd uncovered the existence of a sinister organization called the *Astrum Argentum*—or Silver Star—led by a nefarious mystic called Aleister Crowley. While Crowley pursued an objective of accruing power for the subjugation of humankind, the crew of the airship *Daedalus* had tracked agents of the Silver Star from the U.S. to the Caribbean, then to the wild jungles of the Amazon. There they'd fought a pitched battle, thwarting Crowley's attempt to summon a demonic entity to let loose upon the world. It was only when the ship had limped back to San Diego that Jack had been introduced to Doc's six-year-old daughter Ellen, who had actually been the product of Jack and Doc's love affair in Paris during the war.

It had been a lot for the hotshot fighter pilot to take in, but he adapted well, and the family spent several months traveling together before Ellen's parents were called back to the U.S. to help track down assassins murdering prominent captains of industry. The Silver Star had recovered from their defeat in the Amazon, and had gone straight for the financial backbone of AEGIS. The *Daedalus* crew was reunited, and a dangerous voyage to the Himalayas was undertaken. There, they discovered a valley deep in the mountains, heated by thermal vents, where the world's most toxic plant still grew wild. Again they confronted the Silver Star, and again they limped home, having achieved the slightest of victories.

But now, AEGIS was on the move. Operations had expanded on a global scale, with fully-vetted field contacts around the world and far more resources than before. As if in direct answer to the Silver Star, it was now a complete paramilitary espionage and scientific organization, with a training academy and a new aero-fleet. Field teams were now assigned to preemptively seek out places and artifacts of mystical power, to keep it all out of the hands of the Silver Star.

And that was why Jack and Doc now found themselves underground on a cold Scottish island.

"Goes down quite a way." Doc's voice echoed through the cavernous space.

"Yeah," Jack agreed. "Lots of real estate."

The walls had been carved by hand, like the top slabs, but these sections were closer to seven feet high and probably three to four feet wide. Each wall section held a ceiling slab, supported by two spurs jutting out laterally near the top. The spurs functioned more or less as lintels, bearing the weight of several more ceiling slabs in a row, until the passage gave way to the first antechamber. At this point, the tomb had obviously been carved out of solid rock, as opposed to the quarried slabs used at the entrance. Doc couldn't imagine the sheer number of man-hours such work had taken.

"Whoever is buried here was someone of importance," she said, immediately realizing how stupid the comment sounded.

Jack ignored the invitation to chide Doc for stating the obvious, and played along. "Or someone who really didn't want to be disturbed," he said.

As they ducked through the first antechamber, Doc remembered the lodestone hanging on the leather thong around her neck. She reached down her front collar and pulled it from her shirt, watching as the almost translucent crystal began to emit a soft, blue light—and with it, a harmonic tone. Doc held the strap and let the stone dangle at its end, watching as it twisted slightly and pointed one oblong end into the darkness ahead of them.

Jack shone his flashlight around the chamber, marveling at the garrison of bronze swords, spears and shields lining the walls, now tarnished with a blue-green patina. Whoever resided in this tomb, when reincarnated, would be able to arm a cadre of soldiers, as was expected of the wealthy warrior class.

Doc turned and waved him toward the obstacle which now stood in her way: a round stone slab, carved with intricate Celtic knotwork designs. The lodestone pointed dead center at—or through—the door.

Without speaking, Jack pulled the pry bar from Doc's pack, and levered it under the edge of the four-inch-thick round slab. Leaning to his right, and with Doc's help guiding it along the wall, Jack muscled the giant wheel away from its resting place and revealed another cavernous chamber beyond. He aimed his flashlight into the room and scanned around. It was perhaps twenty by twenty feet, with the oxidized remains of a hundred bronze tools, glazed pottery, and a chariot laying in pieces near the opposite wall. At the center of the room was a hand-carved stone sarcophagus, embellished with a Celtic cross on the top. This was not the simple stone cairn of earlier kings and nobles; this was more akin to Christian burials. That time a millennium ago had to have been one of social and religious transition, at least for this tribe.

Doc stepped through the opening, guided by the blue-white glow of the lodestone, which was now humming a chorus of mystical harmonics. "Okay," she said. "This looks like the main chamber. If our research is correct, the artifact we're looking for is in that stone crypt in the center."

Jack looked dubious. "Of course it is."

"Less sarcasm," Doc instructed. "More crypt-opening."

Jack clipped his flashlight back on his belt and grabbed the pry bar. "Yes ma'am," he said, approaching the stone coffin. "Stand on my left. I'll get the pry bar in a good spot, and we both push on three." He jammed the flat end of the bar between the lip of the sarcophagus lid and its contents, and nodded at Doc. "One... two... three..."

The stone lid scraped away from its thousand-year resting place, sliding over to the side of the crypt before falling flat on the ground with a *thud*. The slight *whoosh* of air filling a vacuum erupted from the open coffin, and the stench of death filled the air.

"Ugh," Jack grimaced. "Stinks to high heaven!"

Doc fanned the smell away from her nose. "Like your socks after we fished you out of that swamp in Haiti…"

"Nice," Jack retorted. "Just keep your eyes out for the item, huh?"

The Pict was remarkably well-preserved for having died in the Dark Ages. Unlike the recently-discovered hill tombs in France, where corpses had been laid to rest in caskets of soft wood, this fellow appeared almost mummified from the cold temperature and having been sealed in stone. He'd been laid in a supine position, arms at his sides, a torc of twisted gold adorned his neck. Jeweled bracelets that looked much too large encircled his wrists, and once-lavish garments of knitted wool and woven flax were broken down and brittle where they held together at all. The bedding he'd laid on for centuries had shriveled to a lumpy gray blanket, frayed and full of holes.

Doc saw it first. A bronze scabbard roughly eighteen inches long lay between the Pict's shriveled, bony fingers and his emaciated thigh. It was engraved in the spiral ocean wave motif of an earlier age. The grip extended up from the sheath in a twist, culminating in the tiny facsimile of a bearded head.

"It's here," said Doc. "They were right. The Dagger of Lir." She tucked the brightly-glowing lodestone back into her shirt and edged closer to the corpse in the open crypt. "Not so legendary as we thought," she muttered under her breath.

Something grabbed Jack's attention, and he stepped away toward the chamber opening to listen. He wasn't sure, but something didn't feel right.

Doc reached delicately into the crypt and removed the sheathed dagger. As she stared at the artifact, she could feel the lodestone thrumming against her chest. As much as she wanted to gaze upon the blade itself, she dared not remove it from the scabbard under these imperfect conditions. Examination was not her assignment; retrieval was.

"You got it?" Jack asked, anxious to get moving.

"It's beautiful," Doc sighed.

Jack waved his pistol at her. "We can admire the fine Celtic workmanship later. Let's get out of here."

Shaken from her trance, Doc quickly stuffed the dagger into her backpack.

"Come on," Jack barked in a hoarse whisper, and then he was gone.

Doc followed, the beam of her flashlight catching Jack from behind. They were through the first antechamber and almost up the stairs when Jack stopped suddenly and pressed himself flat against the stairway. He flagged Doc to do the same. "Hey, Doc?" he whispered, ducking his head below the open tomb entrance.

"Yeah?"

"Remember when I reminded you to bring your revolver?"

"Yes," she assured him. "I have it." She patted the leather holster hanging from her belt.

"Good," said Jack, focused on the windy, wet trail outside the opening.

"Why?" Doc squinted, moving beside him to peer over the stone steps into the night air.

Jack nodded toward the trail from whence they'd come, and breathed a heavy sigh. "Them."

Marching out of the turbulent darkness, only some fifty paces distant, was a whole unit of Silver Star commandos.

- CHAPTER 2 -

Doc gasped and scanned the dark. She could see a handful of men silhouetted by a larger search lantern at the rear of the column. Their squared-off caps and black uniforms were a dead giveaway. The Silver Star had found them.

"Silver Star Commandos?!" she hissed, once again stating the obvious.

Jack nodded. He counted perhaps six or eight of them, but didn't know how many the Silver Star typically assigned to a commando squad these days. Hell, after each major engagement, he always thought they were broken, but they invariably managed to return in far greater numbers, better equipped than before. "They must have tracked us to the island."

He flicked off his flashlight and pointed at Doc to do the same. They didn't want to risk being seen, but he wondered if they'd already observed the falloff from their flashlight beams from below. If they were lucky, the wind and poor visibility would work both ways.

Doc wracked her brain. "But there's only the one map…"

"That we know of," Jack interrupted. "And no kind of cover on this staircase."

In the distance, a male voice barked orders in German.

Doc watched the shapes approach and take up positions on either side of the path, moving eastward across the craggy fields of heather. "They're coming this way," she warned, her voice throaty and panicked.

Searching the field north of their position, he recalled the ancient stone circle. Perhaps he could find cover behind one of the standing stones. It would be a dangerous gamble, navigating treacherous, rocky terrain in the dark.

"Keep your head down below the entry," he instructed Doc. "I'll try to draw them away."

Doc reached to her belt and produced a Colt Police Positive revolver from the leather holster. A recent acquisition, it had a four-inch barrel and walnut grip, chambered for a 38-caliber round. She'd spent a good portion of the winter at the target range, and had found it to have the most power and accuracy of any handgun she could fire without breaking her wrist from the recoil. Holding the gun to her chest, she quietly cocked the hammer back with her thumb and nodded. "I'll cover you."

Jack flashed his half-smile—covering him had been implied. "I'd appreciate that," he answered. Then he scrambled away into the black, wet night.

Doc peered over the lip of the stone slab as the German voices got louder. She knew Jack was headed for the relative cover of the stone circle to the north of the trail, but could make out nothing through the biting wind and icy mist. Then she heard Jack's voice ring out over the weather:

"Hey, wizard wimps! Over here!"

"Oh, dear," Doc muttered. She wondered briefly what he was playing at, but then she saw his flashlight turn on and skitter away from his position into the scrub. The commandos immediately opened fire on the light. MP-18 trench sweepers chattered into the night, kicking up chunks of rock and peaty earth. Their attention had successfully been diverted from the tomb entrance.

Doc took a deep breath, scampered up the steps and ran northward, bent over at the waist. The commandos had concentrated their fire on the rogue flashlight in the heath, but had yet to actually hit it. In its beam, she could just make out a large, masculine form leaning against an ancient granite column fifteen yards away. With the weight of her pack jostling at every step, Doc turned up the steam and scrambled to relative safety next to her partner.

"Nicely done," said Jack. He angled around the edge of the stone and snapped off two rounds. The commando at point cried out in pain and fell to the ground, and the rest of the unit dropped prone. Their commanding officer shouted more orders in German.

"Thank you," Doc answered, raising an eyebrow at him. "'Wizard wimps'?" A round from a stuttering MP-18 sent shards of granite flying past Doc's head. With her back to the stone, she whipped her right hand up past the edge of the monolith and fired upside down, accuracy be damned. A voice cried out—it sounded like the same commando Jack had hit. Ordinarily, she'd be able to muster some compassion for the guy, but right now she just wanted off this rock, and away from everyone shooting at her.

Jack peered into the distant night. "It just came to me," he said, attempting to explain his brilliant nickname for this international gang of occult soldiers. He fired another shot and nodded at the approach of what appeared to be a hovering star. "See that light in the distance?"

The commandos replied with a hail of automatic gunfire, and Jack ducked, pulling Doc's head into his chest. Momentarily distracted by his scent—a combination of sweat and Gold Star aftershave—Doc raised her eyes to look at the light Jack referred to. "Is that —?"

"The *Daedalus*?" Jack finished. "You bet. They're gonna do a pass along the high ground, and we're gonna run for the ladder. Okay?"

Okay? Doc thought. *It's not like I really have a choice, is it?*

"Get ready..." Jack instructed.

Doc moved to a squatting position, readying herself to run for the trail beyond the tomb entrance. "We're going to be thinking up another nickname for the Silver Star. 'Wizard wimps' just won't cut it."

Jack fired another four rounds from the side of the enormous ancient stone, feeling the slide pop back as the last spent shell cleared the chamber. He holstered it and pulled out its twin.

"You just can't comprehend the magnitude of my brilliance," he chuckled.

The hum of electric engines bled in over the wind, and an ominous black shape emerged out of the night sky. It was running in an easterly course, following the main road.

"Steady now..." Jack muttered. "Gotta time this right..."

"That's true," Doc admitted, firing backward again over her shoulder. "Your brilliance is far beyond my comprehension."

Jack aimed a single shot at the search lantern at the back of the commando unit. It exploded with a loud *pop!*

And then the flying machine was upon them.

"Amen, sister," Jack smirked. "Aaaaand *go!*"

They sprinted for the road, negotiating the rutted, treacherous landscape at full speed, in near pitch-blackness. With each step and heavy breath, Doc could hear gunfire behind her—even feel the occasional round whiz by her head as she ran. She trusted Jack and his strategy, but knew it was sheer luck neither of them broke an ankle in some random rabbit hole. The German officer shouted again and they could hear the unit stand and move forward, firing their trench sweepers as they went.

Jack knew they'd need both hands free for the ladder. He holstered his pistols and flagged Doc to do the same, but saw she'd already stowed her revolver.

Before they knew it, the giant shadow was overhead, and the sound of wind had been replaced by the whirring of electric turbofans. Then a metallic clatter erupted behind them— a sound Jack knew to be the ship's aluminum ladder unrolling.

The ladder dragged the ground as the ship surged forward, catching Doc by her backpack. She instinctively reached up and behind with her left hand and grasped a metal rung, kicking to find a foothold as the ladder pushed her forward to collide with Jack. He was ready for the impact, swinging around to the opposite side of the ladder.

"And up we go!" he shouted above the wind, the electric engines, and the hail of bullets buzzing around them like angry bees.

They could feel the ladder ascend with the ship, but knew they couldn't risk merely hanging on and waiting to be hauled aboard.

Doc's arms ached with every rung. "I'm climbing as fast as I can, but we're sitting ducks out here!"

A single rifle shot rang out from the gondola above, and Jack grinned. "Deadeye's got us covered," he announced, nodding above them.

Their stomachs collectively dropped as the engines revved and the ship pulled up, trailing the ladder with it. Soon they were out of range of the commandos beneath them, though now blistered with wind and rain. They felt the ladder's winch mechanism kick in, slowly hauling them upward, toward the giant shadow surfing the night sky.

A light appeared, and a familiar face greeted them as a strong hand extended down from the gondola.

Charlie Dalton pulled Doc into the gondola with a strength belied by a thin, wiry frame. His jet black hair, cropped short, tousled and waved in the wind, some of it matted wet to his sun-browned skin. A Cherokee from North Carolina, Dalton—"Deadeye" as his comrades called him—had been a code-talker in the war, and one of the deadliest marksmen on the Western Front. And of course he'd saved their lives on more than one occasion.

"Gotcha, Doc," he drawled.

Before she could utter an exhausted "Thanks", he'd already helped Jack into the gondola. They stood shivering amidships as Dalton shut off the winch and locked the hatch cover down. Although he'd been out of the Army for a few years, his choice of khaki fatigues, puttees and even casual salutes revealed a man set in his ways.

"Cap'n."

"Hey, Deadeye," Jack nodded, shrugging out of his pack.

"You got the artifact?"

Doc blinked and remembered her own backpack was still weighing on her slight frame. "Right here," she said, slinging the canvas pack to the floor.

Deadeye nodded, not missing a beat. "Good, 'cause Cipher's picked up a mess o' small fighters heading in from the west."

Jack frowned. They were heading west. "We need to skedaddle," he said. "Rivets on the stick?"

"Yessir," Deadeye answered.

"Get topside," Jack ordered. "Cover us with the Hotchkiss."

Deadeye smiled. Shooting things in the air was his second-favorite activity, just after shooting things on the ground. "Aye aye, Cap'n."

Doc grabbed the top of her pack and headed forward, past the crew quarters and toward the main saloon. "Let's go find Rivets."

"After you, Doc," Jack nodded, realizing she'd already left him behind.

They strode with purpose through the galley and main saloon to the forward hatch door. Doc pulled it open and immediately turned to a row of lockers on the right. As she stowed her pack, Jack opened the second door leading onto the bridge. This was a new bird, but everything was just where it'd been on the previous model. The navigation console sat to the right, currently vacant. To the left, a Punjabi woman of twenty-two years in a red AEGIS service beret and headset sat at the radio console. Her blue uniform jacket was in stark contrast to the less formal field dress employed by the others. Jack went directly to the pilot's station at the forwardmost center position.

Carl "Rivets" Holloway turned in the pilot's chair, squinting from under a rumpled gray mechanic's cap and bushy black eyebrows. "It's about time you two showed up," he complained in his gruff, Bronx growl. "What, were you having a picnic?" He slipped out of the safety harness and set the flight controls aside.

"Sure, Rivets," Jack retorted. "In the dark. On a barren rock in the North Atlantic."

"With a squad of Silver Star commandos using us for target practice," Doc added.

Marissa Singh turned from the radio console and smiled. Her raven-black hair was pinned up under the beret, framing a round face and almond-shaped, hazel eyes. A small red *bindi* sparkled from the center of her forehead. "Sounds quite romantic," she quipped in a lilting, posh English accent.

"You have no idea, Cipher," Doc laughed. "He takes me to all the hot spots."

"Well I'm glad you're back," Rivets admitted as he switched places with Jack. "I can fly *Daedalus* in a straight line, but not in a dogfight."

Jack snapped the buckle on the seat harness and pulled the joystick armature in front of him. "Fair enough, Rivets," he said, easing the throttle forward with his left hand. "Get back to the engine room and make sure everything stays ship-shape." As the bristly mechanic in stained coveralls made for the hatchway, Jack turned to their new comms officer. "Cipher, what's the latest?"

Singh lowered her headset and let it hang around her neck. "Last reading I was able to do showed six small aircraft heading toward us from the west, upwards of 100 miles per hour."

"Huh," Jack mused, recalling the first Silver Star fighters he'd ever encountered were war-surplus Fokker D.VIIs. Even with their souped-up engines, they hadn't hit the 100 miles-per-hour benchmark. "Crowley must have sprung for some new planes." He reached into the left chest pocket of his leather jacket and produced a pack of Black Jack licorice chewing gum. Thumbing a piece from within, he removed it with his teeth and replaced the pack in his pocket with a soft pat.

Doc squirmed at her station. "Or conned someone into buying them *for* him," she added.

Jack flipped a few switches on his control panel, and unwrapped the gum from its foil wrapper before cramming it into his mouth. "Buckle up, everybody. This is probably gonna get rough. Cutting all running lights." He knew the incoming fighter planes would be just as blind as he was, up here in the dark, and he didn't want to give them any help.

Before anyone knew what was happening, six Fokker C.V-D fighters were on them. Spandau guns chattered, green tracers and roaring engines buzzed by in the night, to no effect. Jack hauled over on the stick, climbing into a right turn, the thrum of turbofans vibrating through the pilot's console. Every pass they could avoid taking more than superficial damage spoke well of their odds of surviving the night altogether. When the planes came in a second time, he opened up with the forward Lewis machine guns, which did nothing but spit hot red fire into the black curtain of night.

"Drat," he fumed. "They're too fast!"

From behind the pilot's chair, Doc didn't realize how frustrating this exchange was for Jack.

"I'll bet you're thankful for those nose guns AEGIS command added to the new design," she prodded.

Jack throttled forward to full speed. "Yeah, having them linked to the stick is great and all, but night flying means I'm shooting blind." He adjusted their pitch, throttling back down to three-quarter speed. "Doc, get below to the nose turret and take the guns."

Doc didn't need to be told a second time. "Ooh! New toys!" she exclaimed. She was up in an instant, heading for the ladder outside the bridge door.

Cipher raised her headset and positioned it back over her ears. "She sounded far too excited about the new weaponry, Captain."

Jack allowed himself a chuckle. "Yeah, well, Doc's never been one to back down from a fight."

Cipher tapped her left earphone and flashed a look of warning. "They're coming back 'round!"

Jack keyed the *TALK* button on his headset. "Heads up, crew! Evasive action!"

Cipher felt her stomach drop as Jack throttled full speed into a steep spiral climb.

Again the the Silver Star fighter planes swarmed out of the dark, machine guns lighting up the night with tracer fire. The sleek, polished envelope of the *Daedalus* reflected the burning green barium salts in the incoming bullets like a Christmas display. This time, contact was made—bright orange sparks from the port engine nacelle joined the dance of glowing green tracer light.

The attacking plane pulled up to pass, but in doing so, fell into the grips of Deadeye's twin Hotchkiss guns in the top turret. There was a powerful *thud-thud-thud-thud* as the heavy guns spit red tracers and high-caliber lead, shearing off a section of the fighter's bottom left wing. The plane rolled away, speeding off into the dark.

Jack felt the loss of lateral control from the pilot's chair, gritting his teeth. "Uh oh," he grunted. "I've lost port controls!"

Although he'd grown accustomed to the flight characteristics of the prototype light reconnaissance airship—and this new model was even faster and more responsive—there was just no comparison to a modern fixed-wing aircraft. Certainly not six armed ones. And now he'd been hamstrung.

Jack peered out through the panel of bridge windows into a green fireworks display as another pair of fighters came screaming in on them. He fought the stick as the airship limped into the night sky, pushing to the left as the starboard thrust engine overcompensated. A few blasts of red tracer fire spit from the nose turret, but had no effect on the incoming planes.

Suddenly Doc's voice was in his headset. "They're all over us, Jack! I can't get a bead on them in the dark!"

Rivets broke in on the comms. "Looks like they damaged the port thruster!"

No kidding, Jack thought, pressing the *TALK* button on his own headset. "How you looking topside, Deadeye?"

"I winged one," came Deadeye's reply from above, "but there's no visibility out here."

Cipher turned, tuning the radio set with one hand while holding her earphone with the other. "Picking up some interference to the south of us," she announced. "Sounds like an electrical storm."

"Winds really picking up, Cap'n!" Deadeye crackled into Jack's headset.

It gave Jack an idea. He throttled up, and fought the stick against a growing crosswind as he forced the *Daedalus* into a sharp right turn. He keyed the *TALK* button on his headset. "Rivets! How long to bring the port thrust engine back on?"

Rivets returned the expected sarcastic, but entirely reasonable, reply. "Can't be sure until I climb out on the strut to do a damage assessment, And *that* ain't happenin' in the dark, during a dogfight."

Jack was sure he'd known the answer before asking. Still fighting the stick, he muttered, "Then we'll just have to hope for the best." Pressing the *TALK* button once more, he sent a general warning to his crew: "Hang on, everyone!" Grinding his jaws nervously on the gum in his mouth, he pushed the throttle full ahead, turning into the approaching weather system.

Cipher turned at her station, watching him wrestle the flight controls, feet at the rudder pedals, right hand on the stick, left at the throttle. "Captain," she addressed, "are you flying us *into* the storm?"

"Yes, Cipher," he replied with unsettling calm. "Yes, I am."

The crosswinds were now hitting them with the ferocity of a tempest, and the entire airship shook and vibrated as her control systems battled basic physics to keep her on course. Jack found the ballast controls to his left and pressed the *PURGE* button on each one.

Rivets suddenly appeared at the bridge door, red faced and eyes wide. "The heck are you doing, flyin' us *into* a storm with only one good thrust engine?!"

Jack was a cool customer, ninety-nine percent of the time. This, however, was that one percent occasion when he just wasn't having it. "Rivets, either strap in or get back to the engine room!" he barked, setting the mechanic back on his heels. "I need every foot of altitude and as much lateral control as she can muster!"

Chastened, Rivets turned and headed back whence he'd come, grumbling something about being generally unappreciated, and yet being solely responsible for all of them being alive.

Jack's right bicep burned with the exertion of being in a literal arm-wrestling match with his own ship. But the effort was paying off. They hadn't suffered another pass from the fighters, just the occasional stray green light of tracer fire. Finally, as if to give an official seal of approval, Deadeye hailed the bridge. His voice crackled into their earphones.

"Cap'n! Fighters are breaking off! Coming below..."

Cipher tuned her receiver and nodded at Jack. "It's true. Radio chatter says they're heading back to rendezvous..." Her voice suddenly grew faint as she tried to translate garbled voices in German and English. "A carrier... *Osiris?*"

Doc entered the bridge from the turret below, not missing a beat in the conversation. "The Egyptian god of the dead?" she asked.

"History lesson another time, ladies," Jack admonished. "I'm trying to steer us over the storm."

Doc staggered forward as the wind buffeted the tempered windows of the bridge. "Have you emptied the ballast tanks?"

"That was the first thing I did. We need to jettison more dead weight."

Doc grinned. "I thought Rivets was in the engine room."

"I heard that!" The angry Bronx accent erupted over their headsets.

Jack was still Mister Business. He wouldn't be able to relax until he was sure his ship and crew were out of danger. "Spare parts, field gear, anything not nailed down that doesn't help us up here, or in the water."

Doc knew Jack to be a warm, casual jokester when off-duty, but here in the night sky, flying five people into an electrical storm at ten thousand feet—here he was *on*. He was all action, all command, and supremely self--assured in that position.

"Gotcha!" She turned to exit the bridge, recruiting Deadeye as he descended the ladder from above. "Deadeye, with me!"

"Aye aye," the sharpshooter replied, and they were gone.

Jack felt the entire framework of the *Daedalus* creak and moan under the stress of the storm as he desperately tried to push her above it. "You strapped in, Cipher?"

Marissa Singh nodded. "Strapped in, sir."

"Here we go," were the last words Jack Mc-Graw uttered as the airship disappeared into the roiling electrical storm.

- CHAPTER 3 -

As dawn broke silver-white in a gunmetal sky, the *Daedalus* cast a bullet-shaped shadow over the stone villages and mossy green farms of the English countryside. In the daylight, she appeared to have roughly the same profile as the *Daedalus II*, but was sleeker, flatter, with a more shark-like nose than the round lozenge shape of the previous design. The new *Daedalus* was now a class of light reconnaissance airships in the AEGIS fleet, as her registration number LR3-01 signified. The AEGIS "winged sword and shield" insignia displayed proudly from the vertical tail fin.

Like her predecessor, the new ship sported twin thrust engines mounted to armatures on each side, however these were at least fifty percent larger than the last. Two smaller engines fore and aft on each side provided forward and reverse thrust, and the improved aerodynamics had eliminated the need for a lower tail fin. But the technological advances didn't stop there. Her skin of vulcanized aluminum-weave canvas doubled as a passive solar energy collector. Coated with an aluminum powder resin, it wouldn't stop a bullet, but it could stand up to high winds and all types of atmospheric stress.

For Deadeye's beloved Hotchkiss guns, this *Daedalus* had an enclosed ball turret near the dorsal hatch, and one on the nose, under the bridge, equipped with four Lewis light machine guns. She was no fortress, but she could at least defend herself.

A Shropshire man in a tweed cap and rubber Wellington boots glanced up from his flock of sheep, mouth agape. His border collie did the same. The man had only seen one zeppelin in his life, when a Central Powers bombing craft had been blown off course during the war. He'd heard it crashed off the coast of Wales with no survivors. But this vehicle looked smaller and less cumbersome to fly, despite its somewhat slow progress through the morning air. The dog blinked—one eye blue, one silver—and gave a confused bark, and the man simply nodded.

"Aye, Moss," he drawled in his rural tongue. "Looks like a friendly, though I ain't seen engines like *them* on a flyin' machine…"

Not five hundred feet above the farmer and his dog, Rivets sprawled over the port engine stanchion, an aluminum strut that doubled as a plane surface for additional lift. Though he was hooked to a safety cable, this was still hazardous duty. He muttered to himself as he tinkered with the wiring and connections behind the engine access panel, hoping to avoid causing another short.

On the bridge, an exhausted Jack still clutched the controls, as Cipher dozed silently at her station. He could no longer feel his right hand, and a sharp ache radiated from his wrist to his collar bone. Leg muscles burned from six straight hours of rudder control, fighting each and every minute, and dark bags were painted under his eyes. Jack's neck and back were kinked in at least three places apiece, and his beard was now on day three, clearly winning the war of the razor.

Doc stretched, yawning as she found her way back to the bridge. The landscape below was a patchwork of farms, cottages, and one-lane country roads. She approached the pilot chair from behind and gave Jack's shoulder a gentle squeeze. "How you doing, handsome?"

Jack immediately felt the pain in his arm reduce to half its former level. He both loved and feared that she had such a primal narcotic effect on him. "We're out of the storm," he grunted. "Last check Cipher put us somewhere over western England."

Doc let her left hand join her right in squeezing the steel-cable tension out of Jack's shoulders. "This is familiar territory for you," she offered quietly in his ear.

"For us both," he nodded.

Doc smiled. "Yes, but you got to see it from up here."

"True," said Jack, closing his eyes and letting Doc's ministrations release the constricted muscles in his neck and upper back.

She could feel him begin to relax, and when peering over his left shoulder to see his face, she suddenly became aware of his actual level of fatigue. "You look positively beat, honey. Can we find a place to set down?"

"I wanted to make sure we were well out of strike range of those fighters," he replied stoically. "Check with Cipher."

Doc turned to the radio console and approached Cipher with a "Good morning!" which was probably louder than it need have been.

Cipher startled and woke, immediately prodding her stray hair under the red beret. "Huh? Oh, good morning, ma'am."

Doc flashed a smile. She found the way the English accent pronounced *ma'am* as *mom* adorable. "Can you see if there's a place we can set down for some rest and repairs?"

Cipher became a flurry of activity, striding to the navigation console and flipping an oversize book of Ordnance Survey maps open on the desk. Glancing at the clock on the console, she began making calculations in her head: estimating current position based on previous data, plus hours at current speed and heading...

"Yes ma'am," she said finally. "There's the RAF Weston Zoyland airfield in Somerset. I did my aviation training there."

Standing next to Cipher at the nav station, Doc threw a glance down to the pilot's chair. "You know it, Jack?"

He nodded. "Heard of it. Established just a couple years ago, joint U.S. and British." He stretched his legs and turned his attention to his radio officer. "Cipher," he ordered, "contact the airfield and tell them we need a tie-down, some chow, and five bunks. Course setting?"

Cipher used two fingers as an improvised compass, tracing a course on the chart. "Five degrees south-southeast at our current speed should get us there in time for breakfast." She returned to her station and began tapping a Morse code message on the wireless.

A burst of static buzzed in Jack's ear, followed by Rivets' growl. "Well Cap, you got partial power to the the port thruster until we can get to a tie-down."

"Thanks, Rivets," replied Jack, flipping a switch to power on the port thrust engine. He immediately felt the controls even out and begin to cooperate again. "We're heading to an airfield as we speak. You've earned your eggs and toast."

"Just gimme some coffee and we'll call it even."

In that moment, Rivets was every bristly Bronx cabbie, newsie or wise guy Jack had ever met. Doc and Cipher heard it, and it hit them all in the same way. Just like that, the stress of a six-hour storm flight was shattered in the most ridiculous case of the giggles Jack had participated in since he was eight years old.

CR

RAF Weston Zoyland was as modern an airfield as they came. From a thousand feet up, it resembled a massive letter V, with the westernmost runway forming the first arm, and a crowded row of offices, barracks, machine shops and hangars forming the second. A second, longer runway of packed gravel bisected the row of facility structures at a roughly 45-degree angle. Two more unpaved landing strips criss-crossed the lower field. Everything between the two branches of the V was flat, open grass, ideal for smaller planes, balloons and other lighter-than-air craft. Everything outside the runways was Somerset farmland.

The *Daedalus* was cleared to land on the eastern interior field, and towed by a ground crew of burly men to the largest hangar for repairs. The crew disembarked and were shown to a vacant barracks for pilot use: a clapboard room with six metal beds and a writing desk, heated by a cast-iron stove in the center. A metal coffee pot sat atop the stove, and a selection of mismatched camp mugs hung from pegs on a nearby post.

Jack muttered something about sleeping until his name became Rip Van Stratosphere, and promptly collapsed on one of the military cots. He was unconscious before his whole body was horizontal. Doc removed his boots and tucked his limbs under the wool Army blanket, letting him snooze to his heart's content.

Meanwhile, Rivets went to supervise the work in the hangar—being as he was the world's foremost expert on the airship's workings. Deadeye and Cipher wolfed down a quick breakfast in the commissary, then each claimed a bed in the barracks and soon joined their captain in sweet slumber. That left Doc, the only crew member to get any rest during the storm, to her own devices.

She spent the next two hours at a writing desk in the corner, examining the Dagger of Lir, poring over every minute detail in workmanship and decoration, sketching everything in a brand new travel journal. Doc jotted down observations about the possible purpose of the artifact, noting how brightly the lodestone glowed when in proximity. She noted the spiral ocean wave motifs along the blade, which happened to match the designs on the scabbard. And she opined, perhaps without controversy, that the bearded bust at the end of the twisted bronze handle must be a likeness of Lir, the Celtic sea god himself. She made a second set of notes to include with the artifact when they finally delivered it in London.

She was just finishing up her work and packing away the Dagger of Lir, when someone appeared in the barracks doorway and snapped her out of her tunnel vision.

The door swung open and in stepped a slender, dark-haired man with a mustache which looked as though it had been drawn on with India ink. He wore the newly-implemented AEGIS flight uniform: Navy blue trousers with a wide, yellow-gold outer stripe; a cobalt jacket with embroidered patches of rank, special training, and assigned unit; knee-high boots of spit-polished black leather; and a canvas belt which held an assortment of pouches and a holstered sidearm. The cap perched on his head recalled a naval officer design from the Great War—a dark blue top with cardinal-red piping and matching band, and a slim black bill protruding from the front.

"I do hope I'm interrupting something!" the man announced. The posh accent was a dead giveaway, even in England.

Doc turned, eyes wide with joy. "Duke!"

Edward Willis smiled, doffing the officer's cap and stepping into an enthusiastic hug from his former crewmate. "The one and only!"

Jack and Deadeye, now roused from slumber, rushed to greet their comrade. Cipher stirred and stood from her bed, trying to fix the stray locks of hair which had come loose in her sleep.

"Duke!" Jack cried, offering a handshake and a clap on the shoulder. "How have you been?"

Deadeye followed with his own handshake. "Missed ya, buddy."

"Yes, well…" Duke blushed at the attention. "New command and all that."

"That's right," Jack puzzled. "We got the news after the *Daedalus* shakedown cruise that you were leaving for London."

Duke parked a hip on the writing desk Doc had been using, setting his cap nearby. "The whole process went bloody fast. As you know, AEGIS Aviation division put my recommendations into the new *Daedalus*-class light reconnaissance airship—the ones based on the bird you're flying now—and before I knew it, they'd offered me a commission of my own. Meet the new commander of the *Percival*."

Jack couldn't contain his happiness at the news. "The *Percival!* Gee, that's swell, Duke!" He clapped his erstwhile comrade on the shoulder, adding, "Congratulations!"

Doc darted in and left a kiss on his right cheek, causing him to blush a second time. "The perfect English ship for the perfect English commander."

Deadeye was more pragmatic. "We'll miss ya, but dang if it ain't good knowin' there's another *Daedalus* up there, with you at the helm!"

"Oh, *tish*, Mr. Dalton," Duke replied, waving a hand at the very idea. "I say, where's Rivets?"

Jack wandered to the cast iron heating stove at the center of the barracks and poured some coffee from the pot sitting on top. "Over at the *Daedalus*, actually. Supervising repairs." He offered the cup to Duke.

"Uh oh," Duke worried, accepting the coffee. "Nothing serious, I hope."

"Just a run-in with some Silver Star fighter planes." Jack fixed his friend with a gaze that belied the true meaning of his words.

Cipher, in the meantime, had donned her uniform jacket and beret, standing quietly at the rear of Duke's former crewmates.

Duke nodded, letting one of his charming English guffaws loose. "Just like old times, *eh wot?*" Then he spied Cipher, and stood from the desk, handing the coffee to Doc. "Oh, I say! And how is my replacement at the comms performing? Up to par?"

The group of veterans parted and Cipher stepped forward at attention. "Commander, Willis, sir!" she saluted. "Congratulations on your new command."

"At ease, Lieutenant," Duke replied, pronouncing the rank as *leftenant*. He returned her salute and threw a look at Jack and the crew, indicating Cipher. "Came in top of her class, this one. Expert in codes and all forms of electronic communications, fluent in a dozen languages..."

Doc saw Cipher's ears begin to heat dark red. "Duke, stop. You're making the poor girl blush."

Cipher's eyes batted nervously as she gazed away. "You are very kind, sir."

"Stuff and nonsense, Lieutenant Singh," Duke smiled. "You exemplify the best of India, and the best of the Empire."

Jack knew Duke to be a patriot, but any talk even remotely political made him uncomfortable. If it wasn't about a clear-cut case of good and evil, he usually changed the subject. "She's fitting right in, Duke," he assured his old comrade. "But we'll still miss you."

Duke reached for his cap, wistfully trading it from hand to hand. "Well, old boy, time marches on," he said. "In fact, I'm due aboard the *Percival* for our own maiden voyage."

Excellent, Jack thought. *Shop talk.* "What's your destination?"

Duke put his cap on at a rakish angle and smiled. "Cairo."

A hushed excitement suddenly filled the room. Jack cocked his head curiously.

"What's in Cairo?" he asked.

Duke grinned, knowing full well he couldn't share mission details with another crew, close friends though they were. "Apparently, lots of old things waiting to be dug up," he winked, causing a ripple of laughter among the group.

Then the barracks door flew open, and the surly mechanic with a mustache like a Fuller Brush stormed in, apple-cheeked and sweating. "*Where is he?!*"

"As if on cue," Duke replied, bracing himself.

This outburst was new to Cipher; she didn't quite know what to think. The others took it as a friendly hazing and stood aside to watch.

Rivets stalked toward the slender Englishman, sleeves rolled up on his massive forearms. "You didn't think you could get a command of your own and just take off without a proper goodbye..."

"Easy, old boy..." Duke chuckled nervously.

"And leaving me with this Indian radiowoman?" Rivets continued, playing his hand in full. "I mean, she's prettier than you, sure..."

"Yes, hilarious," Duke nodded, grabbing his cap from the desk and waving it like a vaudeville star exiting the stage.

Deadeye raised an eyebrow, eager to get in on the action. "Just prettier?"

"Oh, who am I kidding?" Rivets laughed. "She's just much better at everything!"

Duke put a hand on the stocky mechanic's shoulder, eager to bring this focus on him to an end. "I'll miss you too, Rivets."

"Yeah, well," Rivets stammered, suddenly aware of powerful emotions taking root, "you should get outta here, before I do somethin' sappy... like *hug* ya."

Duke reaffixed his cap to a more presentable position and snapped his heels together. "And on that note, fair winds, Captain." He started to salute Jack, but remembered that neither one of them had worn a military uniform in almost a decade. He offered a hand instead, and Jack shook it.

"Same to you, Duke. Hope to see you up there sometime."

"Farewell, Duke." Doc kissed his cheek again, and everyone crowded around for a farewell handshake.

"Commander," Cipher smiled.

Deadeye landed a playful punch to Duke's shoulder. "Take 'er easy, Duke."

The Englishman smiled, keeping wistful thoughts at bay. As he strode toward the door, he swallowed hard, not letting them see the tears beginning to form in his eyes. These people were his family. They were as one organism, forged in the crucible of the Great War, and bonded through the "Amazon Adventure" of '25, and the "Himalayan Heist" of '26. They'd fought sky pirates and rocket zombies and acolytes of dark magic together. They'd discovered a lost city of ape-men, destroyed a giant zeppelin, and closed a demonic portal. But the threat of the Silver Star had expanded, and AEGIS had expanded to counter it. He had a new crew to break in, and a ship of his own.

Duke turned in the doorway and waved goodbye. "*Au revoir!*"

And then he was gone.

Doc handed Jack the coffee he'd originally poured for Duke. He took it without question, parking his hip on the writing desk as Duke had done.

"I hope AEGIS appreciates what they're getting with Duke in a command of his own," he pondered.

Doc went to the coffee pot to pour herself a cup. "Of course they do. That's why they gave him the job."

"Sure," said Jack, suddenly aware of the other occupants of the room. "Say, what's up, Rivets?"

Rivets appeared to have forgotten the reason for his being present as well, then he snapped his fingers as he remembered: "Oh, we've got about four more hours 'til all the bullet holes in the outer envelope are patched, but the port thruster is back up to snuff."

"Good," Jack nodded. "We'll rest up here tonight and head out first thing in the morning."

"Where to?" Deadeye inquired.

Doc regarded her well-worn satchel, full of notes and the ancient Celtic artifact they'd recovered, lying flat on the desk. She pulled it to her, feeling its weight. "We have to deliver the Dagger of Lir to our AEGIS contact in London. They should have our next orders."

Jack slapped his knee excitedly, setting his coffee on the desk. "Then it's settled! We should find the local pub immediately!" He loved being anywhere but his dry home country during Prohibition.

Cipher spoke up from the foot of her cot. "I know just the one!"

"Everyone follow Cipher," Doc said, shouldering the bag as she pointed the way.

Deadeye shrugged into his field jacket. "Gladly," he murmured to Doc, a twinkle in his brown eyes.

Rivets was already at the door. "Jack's buyin' this time." He held it open as his friends exited.

Jack brought up the rear and was last out of the barracks. "What do you mean, 'this time'?"

The door swung shut. Two cups of coffee sat steaming on the desk in the corner.

- CHAPTER 4 -

It was a small, stone public house dating from the early 1700s, with exposed timbers that showed damage from at least a half dozen fires over the centuries. It may have looked sketchy from the exterior, but inside was warm and dry, and full of real people.

The crew feasted on local Somerset kidney pie and ale, and of course were spotted by a handful of starstruck locals as the heroes from the newsreels. It seemed no one in southwestern England hadn't heard of Captain Stratosphere, dashing American ace of the RFC. Doc watched as Jack made easy friendships with everyone, signing the occasional trading card and accepting every pint that came their way. And when a gruff old

Tommy with one leg and a savage facial scar invited Jack to join him in a few songs from the war, he didn't hesitate.

A portly farmer with a mustache more impressive than even Rivets' Fuller Brush sat on a creaky stool and pounded out song after song, from the jaunty march of "Pack Up Your Troubles" to the melancholy ballad of "The Rose of No-Man's Land". Jack matched the emotional intensity of his one-legged partner, even contributing a beautiful harmony on "It's a Long Way to Tipperary". It was a side of Jack McGraw that Doc had never seen before, and it made her feel warm inside. Or it might have been that third pint of bitter.

They staggered back to the airfield in the dark and collapsed in the barracks for another round of slumber, but this time Jack was awake and alert at 4 a.m., rousting everyone for their flight to London.

The Weston Zoyland Airfield mechanics had worked wonders under Rivets' supervision, patching the breaches in the outer envelope and completing repairs to the port thrust engine. Electric turbofans purred to life in unison as the *Daedalus* rose into the dawn sky and headed east, making excellent time with a tailwind off the Bristol Channel.

Cruising at a solid 80 miles per hour, it took them just under an hour and a quarter to reach Croydon Airport on the southern out-skirts of London, a bustling, modern airfield by comparison to their former accommodations. The greater London metropolitan area was drenched in a spring shower, and the downpour created a patchwork of rainbows around them. As they came in via the north-ernmost landing strip, a brand new De Havilland D.H.66 Hercules buzzed hazardously close, heading off for points east. And it wasn't the only one—Imperial Airways looked to have a fleet of long-range Hercules, along with smaller Avro Andovers for passenger service to the continent.

As much as Jack loved to see consumer air travel growing as an industry, he also knew it would mean the skies were going to get very crowded, very soon.

As the clouds broke and the rain subsided, six ground crew in matching coveralls guided the *Daedalus* in and helped tie her to a mooring mast at the far end of the airfield. Jack and Doc swapped their flight leathers for overcoats and hats to venture into the city. Doc chose a pale green cloche with a white band, while Jack took his black fedora.

They found a town car had been sent to meet them, so they climbed into the back and enjoyed the ride through the West End and Marlborough, to the northeast side of the

British Museum, where their AEGIS contact had an office. While the general public enjoyed access to cultural antiquities pillaged—or preserved, depending on one's political leanings—from the far reaches of the Empire, Jack and Doc were shuttled to the administrative offices, where they would relinquish an artifact of actual occult power. From there, the item would be transferred to the nearest AEGIS Occult Studies division laboratory for examination, and thereafter, crated and cataloged and stored away under lock and key where no Silver Star agent could ever find it. It would never be displayed in the British Museum, or any other museum for that matter, and that was a shame. But it would be beyond the reach of Aleister Crowley and his ambitions.

And that was something, at least.

Colonel Stephen Shaw had been a spy during the Great War, moving from Naval Intelligence to the Secret Intelligence Service as hostilities mounted in 1914. A slender, pale man of 40 years, he was prematurely white-haired, with an angular jaw and a patch where his left eye should have been. The scar that ran from brow to cheek hinted at where the eye had gone, or at least how it had been persuaded to leave. The remaining gray-blue eye shone brightly against his black double-breasted suit. An AEGIS sword-and-shield pin gleamed from his left lapel.

Compared to the rest of the museum, Shaw's office was spartan: a simple 10'-by-15' room with a small desk in the corner, matched with a green lamp from the last decade and a chair dating from the 1890s. In the center of the office was a small table used for examining artifacts. A leaded window allowed some of the gray light of London to peek through.

As they entered, a woman in a dark blue pencil skirt and matching jacket was just turning to leave. "Affirmative," she said, red bow lips visible under her own flowered cloche. She brushed past Jack and Doc as Shaw waved them in.

Greetings were exchanged, and Doc produced her canvas satchel, pulling from within it a heavy yet delicate object wrapped in paper. She set it on the examination table, stepping back to allow Shaw's approach.

"We brought the artifact, as ordered," she said.

Colonel Shaw delicately peeled the brown paper away from the sheath, revealing the finely-detailed Celtic workmanship. "The Dagger of Lir," he almost whispered. "A beautiful and powerful item, from a lost age of magic." He traced a worn finger down one of the bronze spiral designs.

"Pretty sure the Silver Star were after it as well," Jack reported somewhat grimly. "They gave us a run for our money."

"Yes," Shaw replied, his good eye downcast. "Yes, that's not surprising."

Doc could tell that Shaw was distracted. "Colonel Shaw, what is it? What's the matter?"

"I'm sorry, Doctor. My mind is otherwise occupied."

Jack took a step forward, his face a mask of worry. "Anything we can do, Colonel?"

"I'm not sure," Shaw said, waving him off. "Might be nothing."

"What might be nothing?" Jack pressed.

Shaw's brow furrowed as his one eye peered at the two of them. "Well, you see..." he stammered. "The airship *Percival* has just missed another radio check this morning."

Doc's jaw dropped. "The *Percival*?!"

"Duke's ship?" Jack wondered.

Shaw nodded. "You served with Commander Willis, then you know he's a stickler for drill and routine."

"That he is," Jack agreed.

Shaw turned from the exam table and went to his desk, consulting from a small, bound notebook. "The last communique we received was just after midnight, in French air space."

"What did he say?" Doc asked, clearly worried.

"Standard check-in, really," Shaw replied. "Proceeding on mission, nothing out of the ordinary. But one of our contacts at the Marseille Airport reported a flurry of aerial activity from the north directly after communications with the *Percival* went silent."

Jack ran down his mental checklist of ship protocols. "Standard procedure is radio check-in every four hours, by voice or wireless telegraph."

"So as of noon, Greenwich time..." Doc added, doing the math.

Shaw's face was stone. "They've missed three scheduled radio checks."

"You might be able to write one off to a technical problem," Jack offered, "but three means they're in trouble."

Shaw went to the desk and scribbled some quick notes in the tiny notebook. "I'll get these approved today," he explained.

Jack and Doc traded a nervous look, before Shaw tore several pages from the book and crossed the room to them once more.

"Your orders, Captain," Shaw said solemnly as he handed the folded sheaf of papers to Jack. "Track down the *Percival* and effect rescue if you can. If elements of the Silver Star are behind their apparent disappearance..."

"I think that's a given, Colonel," Doc interrupted, her green eyes dark with barely-contained emotion.

Jack opened the paper to see Shaw's signature on a bullet list of the verbal instructions he'd just given them. "Agreed," he said, backing up Doc's assertion. "Safe to say they're back at full strength after the pasting we gave them in the Amazon. Look at their plot to poison prominent industrialists." He scowled, recalling a more recent adventure which had almost cost them their lives. "And our encounter with Maria Blutig in the Himalayas."

Doc nodded emphatically, "If she survived her crash in the Amazon, and Crowley was able to rebuild the *Luftpanzer,* and perhaps an even larger airship... if Cipher was correct about this *Osiris,* it means they've only become better-funded and more politically powerful. We can only guess what their next goals might be."

"Well then," Shaw sighed. "Heaven help us all."

Jack's lips formed a tight line. "Any suggestion where to start?"

"I would follow the *Percival's* course to Cairo," Shaw said. "They've only got a 24-hour head start, but—"

"But a lot can happen in 24 hours," Jack finished. He felt Doc give a quick tug on the sleeve of his overcoat.

"There's no time to lose," she said anxiously. "We'd best be getting back to the ship."

Shaw rummaged through his jacket pocket, producing a fob attached to which was a small ring securing two small, rectangular keys. He threw it at Jack, who caught it in midair. "Take my personal automobile back to Croyden," he said. "It's the red Austin parked across the street. I'll send someone for it later."

Jack wondered what personal feelings Shaw had in the matter, for it was clear he had some. "Yessir," he nodded, not quite saluting as he ushered Doc from the small office into the midday London streets.

The rain had stopped for the past hour and a half, allowing the sun to cook some steam from the sidewalk. Jack shrugged out of his overcoat as they approached a brand new Austin 7 two-seater. Apple-red with a black soft-top, it sported shiny chrome wheel spokes and fenders. Jack went to the left side out of habit, remembering when he opened the door, allowing Doc to slide into the bench seat, that

British cars were made with right-hand drive. "My lady," he said, feigning chivalric intent as he closed the passenger door and went around to the driver's seat.

Jack sat and shut the driver's side door in a single motion, starting the car with a twist of the ignition key and a mighty push of the gas pedal, revving the engine to life. Checking the rear view mirror, he let off the clutch and pulled out onto Montague Street.

The Austin had pluck, that was certain—although shifting with his left hand was an odd adjustment to make. Jack smiled to himself as he accelerated through midday traffic, turning right onto Great Russell Street, then left onto the major thoroughfare of Bloomsbury Street. Cars and horse-drawn carriages competed for precious roadway, with delivery trucks and pedestrians vying for pole-position at the intersections. A red double-decker bus swerved to avoid a black taxi cab that had cut in front, nearly missing the Austin. Jack applied the brakes and gas in equal measure, zipping around both cab and bus. The bus driver honked from his open-air seat at the front as Jack left him in his exhaust.

"We should make the airport in twenty minutes, if traffic keeps this pace," Jack remarked, suddenly noticing Doc's look of perplexity. "What's wrong?"

"I don't know, Jack," she sighed. "This doesn't feel like a normal mission."

Jack gave a self-aware chuckle. "Honey," he said, "normal is not what we do." He negotiated a soft right onto Shaftesbury Avenue toward Charing Cross Road. "If you think about it, crazy and dangerous is all we've ever done. In France during the war, our recruitment into AEGIS, Haiti, the Amazon, the Himalayas..." He glanced in the rear view mirror and hung a left onto Charing Cross. "But two things I know for sure..."

Doc looked up softly. "What's that?"

"One," he said, "there's no one else I'd rather be on the crazy and dangerous ride with." He shifted into neutral, scooped Doc up in his left arm, hoisting her across his lap as he slid toward the passenger side. "Here, take the wheel," he added matter-of-factly.

Doc managed a flustered, "What, why? What's—" as her right hand grasped the steering wheel and she found herself driving the Austin.

"And two," Jack added, "we're being followed."

- CHAPTER 5 -

Jack knew he was right, of course. The black '26 Alvis sedan had been on their tail since the turn onto Bloomsbury.

Doc stepped on the clutch, unconvinced. "How do you know they're following—"

The bark of a Bergmann submachine gun rudely interrupted her, tearing a perforation through the Austin's canvas top.

"I take it back!" Doc shouted, shifting into second gear and flooring the gas pedal.

Jack pulled a .45 from the holster inside his jacket, turning in his seat to fire back at their pursuers from the passenger window. "Hold it steady as you can."

The Alvis weaved left and right as Jack let loose three shots from the Colt, missing with the first two, but hitting the spare tire near the rear of the right-side running board with the third.

Doc saw in the mirror that the gunman was taking aim again, and spun the steering wheel hard to the left, putting another car between them. "We've got to lead them out of the city!"

The Alvis suddenly appeared on their right, and the Bergmann opened up again, punching holes in the body, through the upholstery, and shattering the rear view mirror into sparkling shards.

Doc gasped and screamed as she ducked away from the gunfire. "That was too close!"

The windscreen now sported three holes and a growing spider web among them.

"Turn left up here past the National Gallery," Jack instructed, fumbling his second Colt from its holster, setting the first in his lap.

"Duncannon?" Doc cried. "That's not the way to the airport!"

Jack pulled back the slide on the second Colt and grabbed the first in his left hand. "Would you just trust me, please?" He took a deep breath and closed his eyes in a silent moment of Zen-like focus. "Okay..." Then he launched his entire upper body out of the open passenger window.

Doc was flabbergasted. "What are you going to—you're not actually hanging *out of the window?!*"

Jack took a bead on their tail with each pistol. "It's the only way to get a clean shot!" Then Duncannon Road was upon them, and he shouted over the whistle of spring air and moving traffic, "Left turn! Left turn!"

"Turning!" Doc surrendered her better judgment to Jack's plan and the Austin's suspension, hauling over on the wheel. The small roadster popped up on its right wheels momentarily, and for an instant, Jack had a clear shot at the other driver. His twin Colts blazed, punching holes in the windscreen of the Alvis, and the head of the man behind the glass. Blood painted the punctured windshield and the Alvis veered onto the sidewalk, catching the curb and flipping in a catty-corner somersault, over and over, ejecting the gunman into the air.

As Doc completed the turn onto Duncannon and dropped all four wheels back down, Jack saw the Alvis flip for a fourth time, sailing over the monument to King George IV and coming to a hard landing upside down in the easternmost fountain in Trafalgar Square. The gunman was a pile of trench coat, sundered bones and organs; his landing sent pigeons and people scurrying in every direction. Jack knew both bodies would begin to smolder and decay, withering away to nothing but ash and bone fragments, as all Silver Star agents did when captured or neutralized. It was their calling card. He wished they could go back and check their assailants for such telltales, but the less time they spent in the city, the fewer questions they'd have to withstand from local law enforcement.

Jack returned to his forward-facing position in the passenger seat. Smoke wafted from the warm barrels of the nickel-plated Colts. "Nice driving, Doc."

Doc shook her head in wonder. "Nice shooting, Jack. I knew we kept you around for a reason."

Jack smiled, slipping both pistols away into their holsters under each arm. "You mean aside from my chiseled good looks and rakish charm?"

"'Rakish charm'?" Doc laughed. "Did you read that in a movie magazine?"

"The Valentino cover story," Jack winked, slipping a stick of Black Jack gum from the pack in his pocket.

"I should have known," Doc sighed. "Well, it's going to take more than rakish charm to track down the *Percival* and find out what happened to Duke and his crew."

"Of course," Jack agreed, folding the licorice gum into his mouth. "But it couldn't hurt."

Their laughter was spontaneous and lasted until Doc made a double right turn from Duncannon to Strand. A left on Whitehall put them opposite Parliament Square, and then Millbank to the Vauxhall Bridge across the Thames.

⌘

The girl wore a sleeveless pale blue day dress with a low-slung waist sash and a light wool coat. White patent leather shoes gleaming in the Central Park sunshine, a braided crown of fire-red hair framing her freckled face, she skipped along the path. Her hair and skin tone were her father's—or had been when he was her age. Her mouth and sparkling green eyes were from her mother.

Fast approaching her 8th birthday, the girl was enjoying a day out with her great aunts, whom she'd left a half mile back on the path.

"Well aren't you just the cutest thing?"

The girl stopped in her tracks to see a woman sitting alone on a bench. She was tall, slender, and fashionably dressed in a fur-lined black wool coat, heather-gray pant suit, black leather gloves, and ankle boots. A gray cloche hugged jet black hair bobbed so severely, the edges looked like they could cut someone. Her makeup was equally severe, albeit fashionable, with smoky blue eyes rimmed in thick black liner, and bee-stung lips of blood red.

"What's your name?" asked the woman.

The girl pursed her lips, having already noted at least three potential escape routes and a half-dozen people walking the path nearby. "I'm sorry, I'm not supposed to talk to strangers."

"My name is Elsa," said the woman, flashing a pretty smile. "Now I'm not a stranger."

The girl thought for a moment, eyes narrowing, catlike. Finally she approached the park bench and extended a hand in greeting. "I'm Ellen," she said.

The tall woman shook her hand and looked around the park. "Nice to meet you, Ellen. Where are your parents?"

Ellen grinned. "My parents are... away. They have to travel a lot for their work."

"Really?" The woman's eyes widened. "Are they spies or something?"

Ellen shook her head, giggling. "Nah. Dad's a pilot and mom's a scientist."

The woman leaned back, squinting. "I see. That's very interesting"

Ellen's name rang out from two well-dressed ladies in their fifties, who huffed and puffed as they finally caught up to her.

"These are my aunties, Agnes and Millicent," said Ellen.

The woman stood, towering over the shorter women and young girl by at least six inches. She smiled broadly, shaking each hand and introducing herself. "Well it was so nice to meet you, Ellen. I do hope your parents return well from their travels."

Then she was gone, merging into a crowd of schoolchildren and their teachers.

The two matrons watched her leave, and Millie bent down to look at Ellen.

"Who was that, dear?"

Ellen shrugged.

⋈

They arrived at Croydon Airport with a few more holes in the car than they'd started with, but none in their own bodies, thank goodness. The *Daedalus* was still hitched to the mooring mast at the north end of the airfield, hovering at about six feet, her main port-side gondola door open. A portable, rolling stairway stood on the well-trimmed grass beneath.

The crew had already gathered in the main saloon when Doc entered, followed by Jack. A mix of curiosity and eagerness shone across every face.

"All right, listen up, crew," Jack began. "We have fresh orders from AEGIS and some lost time to make up." He doffed his fedora and nervously spun it in his hand.

Doc removed her overcoat. "Duke's ship has gone silent."

"For how long?" Cipher asked, a pang of concern in her voice.

Jack was already assembling a flight plan in his head. "Just over 24 hours."

Cipher immediately imagined the worst. "Heavens…"

"We just saw him yesterday," Rivets mused.

Jack nodded. "They'd been deployed to Cairo on their maiden voyage."

"So," Deadeye squinted at Jack, "somewhere over France when they went silent?"

"They might have just had a radio malfunction," Cipher suggested.

Rivets knew better. "Not on Duke's watch."

"Even if that were the case," Jack interceded, "they've had plenty of time to make repairs or land in friendly territory to wire in from the ground." Jack shrugged out of his overcoat and draped it over his arm.

Cipher picked up on her captain's use of *friendly territory*, and became worried. "Any Silver Star activity in the area?"

Doc leveled a deadly-serious look at her. "In short, yes."

"Them dang fighter planes?" Deadeye asked.

Jack shook his head. "We don't know for sure," he said. "All we know is the *Percival* has a 24-hour head start, and we need to find her."

Doc nodded. "And rescue Duke and his crew, if possible."

"So how about it, Rivets," Jack raised an eyebrow at his bristly Bronx mechanic. "Is the *Daedalus* ready to burn full speed?"

Rivets straightened to his full five-foot-eight height, thick mustache spreading broadly across his upper lip. "Absolutely, Cap. Give the word."

"Given," said Jack. "Deadeye, take a quick look from the crow's nest, but then you can hit the rack until night watch."

"Aye, Cap'n," Deadeye nodded, heading for the forward ladder.

"Cipher," Jack turned, addressing the young comms officer. "I need your ears to be picking up any possible communication from the *Percival*."

"Yes sir!" Cipher all but clicked her heels, standing straight and exiting toward the bridge.

Jack and Doc noticed they now stood alone in the main saloon, holding coats and hats, about to set forth on another adventure half-way around the world. Doc sneaked in for a kiss, and Jack let her. She wasn't a lover of black licorice in general, but she liked the taste of it from Jack's lips.

"We should wire back home," he said, "let your aunts know we're not coming back as soon as we thought."

Doc agreed. "Ellen should be told. Although I think she got her fill of us over the holidays, and all that flying you did with her."

Jack gave a throaty chuckle. "Girl's gotta learn sometime."

"She just turned *eight*." Doc smiled, noticing that Jack seemed lost in thought. "Hey," she said softly, nudging him with an elbow. "What gives?"

Jack's expression had gone from merry to sour in seconds. He touched her shoulder, looking deeply into her eyes. "Something doesn't sit right about that chase."

"What about it?" Doc asked.

"I know we were on the clock, but why the need for Shaw to have us take his car?" Jack puzzled.

"I don't know," Doc shrugged. "Concerns about local hacks being infiltrated? Faster than taking a black cab?"

"Also bright red and a lot more visible than a black cab."

Doc's eyes widened. "Are you saying Colonel Shaw set us up?"

"I'm saying it doesn't sit well with me."

Doc frowned. He did have a point, and that fact made her uneasy. "What do you want to do?"

Jack gathered their hats and coats together, making ready to stow them. "Nothing just now," he said. "Our orders are legit. If Duke's gone missing, we have to find him."

"So how can I help?" Doc asked.

"You can help me plot his approximate course while I get this bird in the sky."

Doc nodded. She knew they'd have to come back around to Jack's foreboding suspicion, but until then, she was happy to see him clear-headed and on-task.

"Aye aye!"

The giant turbofans spun to life, and the airship *Daedalus* rose gracefully into the skies over London. Coming about to an east-by-southeast heading, Jack kicked the throttle full speed ahead. Each crew member at his station held a silent thought for Duke, and the missing *Percival.*

Jack maneuvered the *Daedalus* as she climbed to an altitude of 2,200 feet. There, he found a nice tailwind and settled in at three--quarter speed. Doc brought a large chart book and stood next to the pilot's station, opening it to display the greater portion of Europe.

"According to Colonel Shaw's mission notes," she began, "the *Percival* was going to set down at Rome to take on provisions."

Jack followed her finger as she traced a line from Great Britain to the Italian peninsula. "London to Cairo is about 2,100 miles," he factored. "Rome is just over nine hundred. That's almost a halfway point."

Doc frowned. "Although, on a maiden voyage, don't you think Duke would have broken it up a bit more?"

Jack reached over, altering Doc's line with his own index finger. "I would probably opt for Rome, east to Athens, then drop down to Cairo."

"The course makes sense," Cipher acknowledged. "That's all AEGIS-friendly airspace."

Doc returned to the nav station as Jack keyed the *TALK* button on his headset. "Deadeye, how's it looking topside?"

"All clear, Cap."

Jack hit the button again. "All right, Charlie. Head on down and get some shuteye. Relieve me at zero hundred hours."

Deadeye's monotone crackled into Jack's ear. "Affirmative."

"And Rivets," Jack added, hitting the button a third time, "I need every kilowatt you can squeeze out of those engines."

"You got it, Cap," came the reply, along with a burst of static.

"Hang in there, Duke," Jack McGraw said quietly to the clouds beyond the bridge windscreen in front of him. "We're on our way."

- CHAPTER 6 -

The woman made her way back to the Hotel Belmont on Park Avenue, stopping briefly at the front desk to check her messages. There was one: a single telegram in a sealed Western Union envelope. She thanked the bookish desk clerk and retreated to her room on the 6th floor.

Slitting the envelope open with a manicured fingernail, the woman opened the folded telegram and read. It would have looked like gibberish to the casual observer, but she knew better. It was in code, and she happened to have the weekly cipher committed to memory.

MARIA—

CONTACT SCHWARZHUND IMMED.

—A.A. CMD

Black Dog? She thought. *What could Captain Hummel possibly want with me? Especially in light of his recent failure in Shanghai...*

Maria Blutig went to the hotel room closet and opened it, lifting a large wooden box with a leather handle onto the writing desk next to the wall. Flipping open the latches, she pried the two halves apart into a V, revealing a long-range field radio set. She flicked on the power, tuning the dial to the predetermined frequency, setting the wired transmitter next to a pad of notepaper and pencil. She began tapping out a message in the code cipher she'd just used to figure out the telegram.

WOLF MOTHER TO A.A. CMD—

POS. I.D. MADE ON ELLEN STARR.

CALLING BLACK DOG BY REQUEST.

She prepared to wait, but the reply was almost immediate:

BLACK DOG TO WOLF MOTHER—

RENDEZ. CASSINO ITALY.

HAVE GIFT FOR YOU.

She wondered what Ernst Hummel had that she would consider a "gift", but then she really wasn't in a position to question anything. Since her failure to protect the base at the Eye of the World in the Himalayas the previous year, Maria had found herself in Aleister

Crowley's doghouse. Displaced from her privilege within the Silver Star organization as Crowley's most trusted second-in-command, she'd been cut off from all but the most perfunctory communication with him, deprived of his counsel. She maintained her rank and her reputation within the greater organization, but Crowley's favor—and his heart, it seemed—were closed to her.

It made her profoundly sad to remember the days when she could share his bed, administer his heroin injections, and bask in his affection and the glow of his arcane essence. For they had shared more than sex and intoxicants; they'd shared a powerful, mystical bond. Maria desperately wanted that connection back. Back in his favor. Back in his heart.

She dabbed a single tear from her powdered cheek and resolved to take advantage of the opportunity *Schwarzhund* was offering. She knew Captain Ecke was in the North Atlantic, heading to Nova Scotia to deploy some covert agents, and she was certain she could figure out a rendezvous. Ecke still owed her for championing the commission of the *Luftpanzer II* after its predecessor's fiery destruction in the Amazon. In fact, Crowley had been reticent to invest the resources into any more such grand weapons of warfare, but Maria had petitioned The Master with reason and ingenuity, the result of which was both the *Luft-*

panzer's replacement and the supercarrier *Osiris,* flagship of the Astrum Argentium aerofleet.

And word had only recently come across the grapevine that Captain Hummel, the infamous Black Dog of the Silver Star's Asian operations, had been removed from his command of the naval cruiser *Silver Shark* following the disastrous failure of "*Projekt Abheben*" in Shanghai. Maria wondered how he'd managed to ascend to the command of the *Osiris.* Failing upward wasn't something usually seen in the Silver Star. If a commander botched an important assignment, it was not unusual to disappear altogether, fodder for The Master's power pool. However, if one made a particularly compelling case to Crowley, sometimes he'd end up putting you where you most needed to be to make it up to him.

Shame was a powerful tool within the Silver Star, and one Crowley used expertly.

Maria had always been suspicious of Hummel, and jealous of his rapid rise within the organization, but in his transmission she sensed an opportunity for easy alliance that could benefit them both. She would hitch a ride on the *Luftpanzer II* and meet the Black Dog in Italy. She would see what "gift" Hummel had for her, that she would be able to leverage into a new future and a return to The Master's good graces.

℥

It was nearly 5 p.m. when Doc woke from her afternoon sleep and made her way to the bridge. The sun was setting behind them and the segmented windows showed a dark blue sky above pockets of lights on the ground below. Cipher tended her radio receiver while Jack kept *Daedalus* pointed on course.

Jack heard her boots on the bridge deck plates and welcomed her forward. "Heya, Doc."

Doc yawned and leaned over the pilot's chair, draping her right arm around Jack's neck and shoulder. "Did I miss Paris?" she asked sleepily.

"Two hours ago," Jack said. "Looked nice in the afternoon sun." He rested his head back in the crook of her shoulder. "We'll have to take a vacation, go back sometime..."

Doc giggled, lips bussing his ear as she stood upright to take her station. "Captain McGraw, the last time we visited Paris together, we ended up with a daughter."

Jack feigned surprise. "You don't think that would happen again, do you?"

"Should I leave you two alone?" Cipher insinuated with a sideways glance.

All three shared a laugh as Doc sorted through her charts.

"Please don't," she warned. "We have a habit of getting into trouble when we're left alone."

Jack raised an index finger. "To be fair, we get in trouble when we're *not* alone."

"True," Doc nodded, unrolling a chart of central Europe. "Say, what's your current position?"

"Just shy of the Swiss border," Jack replied. "Less than a hundred miles west of Zurich."

Doc found their location on the chart and marked it with a red wax pencil, consulting her watch and making a quick calculation in her head. "Making good time," she observed, impressed.

"I tell ya," said Jack. "The improvements they made on this new model..."

Cipher cut him off. "Captain, I'm picking up a severe weather system moving in from the northeast. And a great deal of radio chatter."

Jack frowned, peering through the windscreen to port. There was indeed a gathering of ominous gray-black clouds illuminated from within by the flicker of lightning. "What is it, Cipher?"

Cipher turned, holding one earphone to her head, listening intently. "It's a mix of German and English. And it's on a frequency used by the Silver Star aero-squadron we encountered over Scotland."

Doc's jaw dropped in astonishment. "They can't have found us..."

Jack wasn't about to be caught off-guard again. "There's one way to find out," he said, throttling to half speed to reduce the drain on the battery array. "Give me a radio detector reading, Cipher."

The young woman nodded and powered the detector on, eyes widening as the familiar *deet-deet-deet-deet* sound of the reflected radio waves hit the sensor. "What...how?" she gasped. Several blips were clustered on an intercept course.

"I don't like this," Doc muttered.

Jack turned in the pilot's chair, a crimson flush rising to his face. "Talk to me, Cipher."

"Three...four...no, *six* small craft, Headed right for us."

Doc keyed the *TALK* switch on her headset. "Deadeye, we need you topside—on the double!"

Jack fished a stick of gum from his pocket and crammed it into his mouth, furious at being caught unaware. "Where the devil did they come from?"

"They appear to be hugging the storm," Cipher explained, feeling entirely inadequate in her response.

Doc shook her head, bewildered. "Pretty risky flying."

"Downright crazy," Jack offered, "and genius."

Doc could understand a certain level of admiration coming from Jack. He respected unconventional thinking, and unconventional flying. Still, this made no sense. "But they couldn't have just come out of the storm," she protested. "They had to launch from some—"

Cipher broke in, pressing the right earphone to her ear. "The small craft are being coordinated from...a larger craft riding the top of the system."

"Larger craft?" Jack repeated, already putting the puzzle together in his head.

Cipher turned and looked at him, her face a mask of worry and alarm. "*Much* larger."

"Cease radio scan," Jack ordered, immediately throttling the engines ahead full.

"What are you going to do?" Doc asked.

"I'm putting the engines at full speed and we're gonna try to outrun this storm."

Doc's brow furrowed. "At least it's not nighttime yet," she sighed. "Still have some visibility. I'll get to the nose turret."

As she left her chair to head toward the bridge door, Jack threw a quick "Thanks" over his shoulder, then hit the *TALK* button on his radio. "Deadeye, you in the nest?"

A burst of static was followed by the Cherokee's cool baritone. "Heck of a storm blowing in, Cap. You say there's a ship in there?"

"*On top* of it," Jack corrected.

A brief moment of silence was followed by another static burst and: "I don't see any— wait a minute. Well skewer me with a froggin' fork."

"What do you see, Charlie?" Jack demanded.

"I see that Crowley has a thing for real big airships. This thing's gotta be twice the size of the beast we engaged over the Himalayas."

He wasn't far off. The *Osiris* was larger than any rigid airship that had flown before. Gleaming black atop the flickering lightning below, she was a monster of modern engineering: built like a catamaran, with a torpedo-shaped envelope on either side of a flat topdeck used for launching and receiving her nest of fighter planes. Perhaps 1200 feet in length and 500 wide, her aft quarter was an aerodrome with an air control observation tower sprouting from its center. A number of outboard thrust engines burning diesel churned in the distance. Even miles away, Deadeye could see she was bristling with heavy guns.

As the static *crunch* signaled the end of Deadeye's transmission, Jack hit the *TALK* button in response. "I'd say so, if it's carrying a squadron of six fighters."

Cipher was beside herself. "How are they always right on top of us?"

Jack had to acknowledge a creeping gloom. "That's a really good question that I hope we have the opportunity to answer someday," he said with a sigh.

Suddenly Charlie's voice burst back into his ear. "Fighters are closing, Cap."

"Fire a warning, Charlie," Jack ordered. "Keep 'em off our tail."

Topside, the twin Hotchkiss guns stuttered their basso song, spitting red tracer fire into the sunset. The two lead fighters split off to either side of the fleeing dirigible.

Doc's voice was next on the comm channel. "Jack, we won't be able to take six fighters with this armament…"

"Don't worry," he replied as he keyed the *TALK* button on his headset. "I don't intend to to get suckered into a fight."

Cipher turned in her chair. "But we can't outrun these new planes—"

"We might not need to," Jack shot back over his shoulder, "if we can *outclimb* them."

Engines whined full ahead, with the stick urging the bullet-shaped airship into a steep, angled ascent. Cipher recalled her flight training in Navy surplus airships.

"But sir," she warned. "If we ascend too high—"

"It's okay, Cipher," Doc assured over the radio. "Jack knows what he's doing."

It was true. The young officer watched as Jack negotiated the flight path of the *Daedalus*, snapping commands over the headset as he flew.

"Rivets, double-check all exterior windows and hatches. Once we hit 12,000 feet, go ahead and hit the O-2."

"Affirmative, Cap," came Rivets' static-filled reply.

Without addressing Cipher directly, Jack explained over the comms. "One of the improvements to this new design is a pressurized gondola." He paused, then added, "I do read the technical manuals, y'know."

Doc's voice breathed into his ear. "Just one of the reasons I love you."

"What about Deadeye?" Cipher asked, concerned.

Jack continued in the climb. "The turrets are enclosed and heated, and have oxygen piped to a breathing mask," he said.

With the ship's current incline, Deadeye had an expansive view unobstructed by the tail assembly. As they struggled through the storm, he could see the black Fokker C.V-Ds swarming in pursuit, occasionally snapping short bursts from their Spandau machine guns.

He hit the *TALK* button on his headset. "They're firing on us, but it looks like they're out of range. Not giving up, though."

Jack squinted through the flashes of lightning and droplets of rain collecting on the bridge window array. "We need to get above the storm," he broadcast to the crew. "We have no idea what the ceiling is on that new carrier."

"Altitude 10,800," Cipher chimed in.

The *Daedalus* bucked and shuddered against the savage crosswinds. Jack struggled with the stick. It was all he could do to keep her on course and climbing. "Come on, sweetheart," he muttered.

Deadeye watched as the fighters pulled within weapon range, letting loose with green tracer fire. "They're comin' in!" he warned into the radio, returning red incendiaries, the tracers reminiscent of flashing Christmas lights.

Cipher watched the altimeter at her station. "Eleven thousand."

Jack leaned in the chair, clutching the joystick with white knuckles. "She really wants to fly..."

Doc burst into Jack's headset. "I can't get a decent shot unless they pass in front of us."

"It's okay, Doc," Jack assured her. "That's what those nose guns are for. Just wait 'til they come to you."

Then the two lead C.V-Ds were on them, all roaring engines and barking guns.

- CHAPTER 7 -

"Taking hits to the outer envelope!" Deadeye's voice was elevated and more animated than Jack was used to. But he didn't need his gunner to tell him they were taking hits. The rapid *tink-tink-tink* of machine gun rounds hitting aluminum struts was enough of a clue.

As the two fighters peeled away and made room for the next two, Rivets found it necessary to curse into the comms. "Blasted sons of —"

"Cut the chatter, Rivets!" Jack spat. "I'll throw some evasive maneuvers into the climb. That might keep those fighters at arm's length."

Stomachs fell as the *Daedalus* rolled over in a corkscrew pattern, still climbing ever higher above the storm system. The second wave of fighters opened up with their glowing green machine gun fire, but all shots went wide of the target.

"Doing the trick, Cap!" Deadeye observed from the dorsal turret, wanting desperately to spend Hotchkiss rounds at the attackers, but adhering to his uncle's advice on shooting: *Never pull the trigger unless you're pretty darn sure you can hit what you're aiming at.*

On the bridge, Cipher kept the altitude tally. "Twelve thousand…"

"Rivets, hit the oxygen," Jack ordered, and almost immediately the hiss of compressed air filtered into each station.

"O-2 is flowin' Cap!" said Rivets over the comms.

Deadeye reported from his turret. "Fighters are still on the chase."

The *Daedalus* shuddered and rattled in the sky, and Jack felt the approach of a tailwind. "Whoa there!"

Cipher looked worried. "What is it, Captain?"

Jack shook his head. "Ran into a whole new wind current. Adjusting to take advantage of the extra push…"

As they pulled above the storm into the cold evening sky, Deadeye watched the fighters bank and head back toward the *Osiris*. "Fighters breaking off, Cap'n!" He finally announced.

"Stay sharp, Deadeye," came the captain's reply.

Cipher visibly relaxed in her chair with a sigh of relief.

Jack's face was a granite mask. "Oh," he said, "we're not finished yet."

CR

At every duty station, ears popped as the *Daedalus* climbed into the late afternoon sky.

Deadeye reclined in the dorsal turret and watched filmy clouds part to reveal a low sun and, through the dusky haze, a scattering of stars across an inky blue sky. He inhaled slowly through the oxygen mask connected to the air feed. He knew in his gut this was higher than they'd flown before—even in the Himalayas.

On the bridge, Jack monitored the ship's altitude and controls, impressed. He keyed the *TALK* switch on his radio. "Rivets, the new gas mixture is really doing the trick."

He referred to the recently-introduced hybrid lift gas now employed in all AEGIS airships. As recently as the previous year, it had been an innovation the Silver Star was willing to murder for. The eccentric industrialist and AEGIS backer J. Elling Ponderby had been working on the formula for the lift compound, and had almost succeeded. Assassins killed Ponderby with a potent toxin which essentially cooked his tissues from the inside out. Doc had witnessed the assassination, unable to render any aid or comfort to the man as he died in agony. The search for the botanical source of the toxin had led the *Daedalus* crew far into the Himalayas, to a secluded thermal valley at the top of the world where they'd fought a pitched battle against the Silver Star, both in the sky and on the ground. Though seemingly a stalemate, the venture had been a tactical success, as the *Daedalus* crew had overcome seemingly impossible odds and escaped with their lives, while shutting down access to the poison, permanently.

Thomas Edison, not being a man who responded well to the word "can't", took Ponderby's corporate chemistry research and, within six months, AEGIS Aeronautics division had solved the ratio for the combination of hydrogen and helium (with some help from Rivets and Duke). Then the prototype *Daedalus II* had been decommissioned to make room for the *Daedalus III* and *Daedalus*-class light reconnaissance airship—the craft which would become the backbone of AEGIS operations worldwide.

Though there was no *III* in the ship's nameplate, Jack was aware that, aside from the original *Daedalus* built and flown only by original inventor Vincenzo DiMarco, he had captained the first of each iteration of the aircraft. It was an honor, and a responsibility. As much as he was a fighter pilot at heart, and loved the speed and response of a good plane at his command, he had grown to love each version of the *Daedalus*. He knew each ship like the back of his hand, and had a way of eking out speed and performance far beyond the official technical parameters. Now he was pushing the boundaries of altitude.

Doc entered the bridge, finding her seat at the navigation console. "Good ol' AEGIS Aeronautics division," she quipped, adding, "What's our current altitude?"

"28,000 feet," Jack announced, a hint of wonder in his tone. "And she could probably go higher."

Cipher turned to face them. "That's two thousand feet above the official service ceiling," she warned.

"As long as we're out of range of those fighters," said Doc.

Jack squinted through the windows into the moonlit night sky. The nearest cloud layer floated nearly a mile below them. "Well, the bad news is," he began, "this isn't like the war, when fighters were stalling out at 10,000 feet and an airship could simply climb out of range. These new C.Vs have a much higher ceiling..."

"About 19,000 feet," Cipher added.

"About 19,000 feet," repeated Jack.

Doc was pretty sure she knew the answer to her next question, but she asked it anyway. "So how do we handle them?"

"Endurance," answered Cipher.

Jack snapped his fingers. "Give that gal a prize. As long as planes still run on liquid fuel, they have a finite range. Our all-electric power plant and drive system means we can outlast just about anything in the sky."

Doc thought of the carrier they saw and suddenly wasn't convinced. "Including the *Osiris*?"

Jack rubbed his jaw, bristly with several days' beard. "Now that does throw an interesting wrinkle into the situation," he said, musing over tactics and organization. "But consider that they have to carry fuel and personnel for a squadron of planes, plus ground troops, gunnery and ship's compliment, and food and water for all. Their—we'll call it their 'resource consumption rate'—is much, much higher than ours."

Cipher frowned. "They must have a friendly port somewhere in central Europe."

"It's the Silver Star, Lieutenant," Doc huffed. "They have friendly ports all over the globe."

"But *how?*" Cipher shook her head, bewildered. "What is the *appeal?*"

"Power," answered Doc, resolute. "Unfettered and unimaginable power."

Cipher simply couldn't picture anyone in their rational mind taking such weak bait. "We have all of the latest technology—"

"That definitely has its place in helping the struggle against evil," said Doc. "But never underestimate the appeal of power."

"Crowley can't possibly follow through on such promises, can he?"

"And you've just solved the equation, Cipher," Doc smiled. "You're absolutely right. Crowley has no intention of giving away the power he's accumulating. He parcels it out to a few trusted generals in the field, and always a bit less than he keeps for himself. The display of power by his generals maintains a sense of awe and the promise of more for the rank and file."

Jack yawned silently, popping his ears to equalize with the cabin pressure. "I almost feel sorry for those poor mooks at the bottom, but they chose to be there."

"For the most part," Doc corrected.

Jack nodded, chastened. "Point taken."

He flipped some switches on his control panel and keyed the *TALK* button on his comms. "Rivets, ready on the O-2 tanks. Taking her back down to cruising altitude."

"Aye aye, Cap," came the crackly reply.

Stomachs fluttered as valves vented lift gas into the atmosphere and the *Daedalus* began her descent. Jack cocked an eyebrow, knowing no better than any member of the crew what awaited them on their course.

"Next stop," he said, "Rome."

- CHAPTER 8 -

Commander Edward Willis blinked and tried to shake the dust from his brain, to no avail. It was nighttime—that much he could tell through the window of his quarters. Or perhaps his captors had curtained the windows from outside. His arms and shoulders ached, but he wasn't sure why.

He vaguely remembered losing navigational control when he'd turned away from the storm. Something much faster than the weather had overtaken them. Brief flashes came to him like a photographer's bulb, overloading his dulled senses: the hollow sound of the *Percival*'s envelope punctured by harpoons and grappling cables; the scream of electric thrust engines as he'd throttled full speed to escape; the pop and hiss of gas grenades dumped from the top hatch.

Duke recalled the sickening groan of aluminum struts as the *Percival* had been reeled in like a swordfish on a sportsman's line.

Now, the electric turbofans were silent. The steady monotone of massive diesel engines pulsed through the deck plates of the *Percival*, into Duke's knee-high leather boots. He found it oddly calming. But then he remembered his precarious situation and decided not to give in to the almost hypnotic white noise coming from below decks. The sound and motion told him the *Percival* had likely been rafted to a larger vessel, and it was now being towed—or carried—to their destination.

Shaking his head once again, Duke tried to focus. He realized another reason for the soreness in his arms was due to his being shackled with chains that ran through a hastily-installed circular screw eye in the ventilated floor. He became aware that he was seated in the chair associated with his sleeping quarters, the one usually parked at the small writing desk next to his bunk. He pulled at the manacles, testing them. The attached chain dropped down toward the floor, through the O of the hardware screwed into the deck plate, and terminated at an identical pair of cuffs at his ankles. Duke felt the metal tug at his legs as he pulled upward with his hands. This would not be an easy escape. Of course, it would be downright impossible if he couldn't get his head clear.

Whatever knockout drug the Silver Star was using was nothing like any other intoxicant he'd sampled, knowingly or otherwise. He hadn't been injected that he could recall, so his current mental haze was most likely an after-effect of the gas. Of course, it could just as easily be some kind of slow-acting poison, which their agents were known to use. But he'd never discover which, bound to the floor in his quarters.

Clamping his eyes shut, he took a slow, deep breath and quietly exhaled, gathering whatever faculties he could muster. His eyes fluttered open as he made note of booted footsteps on the gantry outside.

The door to the tiny room opened, and he saw a familiar silhouette blocking the way.

"Guten Abend, Commander Willis," said a woman's voice, dripping with equal parts venom and delight.

Good God. Not her. Duke shuddered and shut his eyes again, praying for his nightmare to be over.

℈

They came down out of the Alps as the sun hung low in the western sky. The 200-mile trip almost due south took them just over two hours, benefiting from an intermittent tailwind. The ancient city of Rome, once the hub of civilization within the known world, was now criss-crossed in a spiderweb of telephone, telegraph, and electrical cables, sparkling with artificial light and choked with motor traffic. Italy's role in the Great War had bought them annexes of Tyrol and portions of the Dalmatian coast, at the cost of more than half a million lives on their side alone. And now Italy's once noble people suffered—five years and counting—under fascist totalitarian rule.

Rome was supposed to have been a friendly harbor for AEGIS operations, supported by industrialists, scholars, and even the Vatican. Yet as the *Daedalus* descended over Ciampino Airport outside the city, that notion would be put to the test.

Jack left Rivets in the pilot's seat, with instructions to keep the turbofans idling in case a quick getaway was needed. Cipher stayed at her station, monitoring radio chatter. Doc and Deadeye joined Jack as he unfolded the segmented stepladder from the floor panel inside the port gondola door and hopped down onto the tarmac.

The sun was dropping beneath the city skyline, leaving the airfield illuminated by little more than a few stadium lights and the amber glow of the administrative office and flight control booth. Jack instinctively shucked one of his nickel-plated Colts from its holster and checked the clip.

It was Doc who first saw the trucks. "Oh, look who's coming to meet us," she sighed.

Two war surplus troop trucks rattled and puttered across the overgrown gravel runway, headlights isolating the three aeronauts in their beams. They sounded uncharacteristically ill-maintained, if in fact they were military vehicles. Of course, they could have been the only trucks available in the motor pool, especially if the occupants were in a hurry.

Deadeye squinted and was somehow able to see past the white blur of truck headlamps. "Heads up, Cap'n," he warned. "I remember those uniforms."

Jack's eyes narrowed as the trucks came to a squeaky halt about thirty feet away. "Mussolini's secret police," he muttered, recalling a time when they'd been little more than racist thugs causing mayhem in the streets. Thugs he and Deadeye had encountered more than once in their postwar adventures.

"I don't like this," said Doc.

"Neither do I," Jack agreed. "Deadeye, hop up in the gondola to keep us covered, will ya?"

"Don't gotta ask me twice." Deadeye nodded and disappeared into the ship, taking up position just inside the open door with his trusty Winchester repeater.

A dozen paramilitary troops in long coats and round, gray *beretto* caps piled out of the trucks and formed a semicircle. Jack and Doc could see long 9mm clips extending from the tops of their guns—probably OVP automatic rifles, Jack reasoned. He'd seen some original Beretta 1918 rifles in action shortly after the war, and he knew they were deadly at short range.

The arc of troops parted in the middle as a tall officer in a leather trench coat stepped out of the cab of the lead truck and moved toward the Americans.

Jack decided he wouldn't take any unnecessary risks, so long as this officer was reasonable. "*Buona sera, signore,*" he greeted with a slight military bow.

The officer didn't return the gesture. He simply removed his leather gloves, tucking them into his belt. For the first time, Jack noticed the pin on the officer's jacket was a captain's rank insignia.

"*Buona sera,*" the captain replied. "Papers, please."

Jack reached into his inside breast pocket and produced the crew passports and AEGIS documentation for the *Daedalus*. He noticed the captain seemed to be thoroughly disinterested in the people standing in front of him and more on the airship hovering three feet above the landing strip. He handed over the documents and nodded. "Here you go. I'm Jack McGraw, captain of the airship *Daedalus*. This is Doctor Dorothy Starr."

Doc smiled and waved a bit too warmly. "Hello."

"How many in your crew?" inquired the captain, giving the passports a cursory glance with dark, shifty eyes. He had a receding hairline made prominent by too much hair grease, and a gaunt, cruel face. He looked like the textbook kid who'd been picked on in childhood and had grown into the nastiest bully on the block. Doc put him at about 40, with the bearing of someone from money who'd been stiffed on a promotion during the war and was now weaseling his way up the ranks in Mussolini's goon squad.

"Five, including myself," answered Jack.

"What is your business in Italy?"

"We're on a rescue mission, actually."

This is good, Doc thought. *Maybe Jack can engage his sense of self-importance and enlist his help.*

Jack shifted his weight. "We're looking for Commander Edward Willis of the airship *Percival*..."

"You will power down your engines."

Doc blinked. Jack hesitated, thinking maybe he hadn't heard the captain correctly.

"I'm sorry?"

The captain was resolute. "You will power down your engines, and have your crew disembark the ship."

Doc wasn't used to being in any kind of official trouble. "But why?" she asked.

The captain looked them both in the eye for the first time. "You are being detained on suspicion of espionage."

"Espionage?" Doc repeated, aghast.

"Here it comes..." Jack muttered, knowing how government officials loved to tie people up in their red tape. Even if AEGIS headquarters wired a considerable bribe, this could put them seriously behind schedule.

"Your aircraft is to be confiscated and examined."

Doc flushed nervously. "There must be some mistake..."

Jack put up a hand to get the captain's attention. "*Signore*, we are from the Allied Enterprise Group for International Security, looking for one of our ships." Since the founding of AEGIS, the A had stood for "American", but now that it was a truly worldwide endeavor, the wording had been altered to reflect that, without having to change the acronym.

"You are spies," the captain said matter-of-factly, "and enemies of the Italian state."

The rustle of a dozen weapons being aimed was drowned out by Jack's thumb cocking the .45 he suddenly held at the face of the captain. The barrel nudged the crevice between the man's forehead and the bridge of his nose. The captain froze, not in fear, but quiet understanding.

"I was really hoping not to do this," Jack said, taking the crew documents back and handing them to Doc. "But I have one of the best marksmen in the world taking aim at your head, *Capitano*..."

"Terenzi."

"*Capitano* Terenzi," Jack repeated, backing away a step, moving Doc with him.

One of the soldiers pulled back the bolt on his rifle, and Jack stepped forward again, angered yet supremely calm. The barrel of his Colt went right back to the bridge of Terenzi's nose.

"Tell your men to drop those trench sweepers."

Terenzi actually flinched, eyes widening. He saw Jack was serious. "*Cadere i fucili.*"

The clatter of twelve rifles hitting the gravel simultaneously was impressive. These goons were highly trained.

Jack stepped back again. "Now, Doc and I are gonna climb aboard our ship and be on our way, and if you're good little fascists and stay put, no one need be shot." He stood by the open door of the gondola, pistol still aimed at the captain. Deadeye knelt inside, keeping watch down the sights of his Winchester. Jack waved Doc aboard.

"After you, Doc."

"Way ahead of you," said Doc, scampering up the folding step and into the gondola.

As Jack prepared to follow, Terenzi addressed him from the center of the troops. "*Signore* McGraw," he called, "I will see you die."

Jack saluted from the step. "Maybe so, Terenzi. Maybe so. But not here, and not on such a beautiful evening." He nudged the Cherokee marksman in the ribs. "Deadeye, if just one of these mooks goes for a heater, you have my permission to air 'em out."

The man with the Winchester smiled. "Yessir."

Doc called from inside the main cabin. "All aboard!"

Jack hailed the secret police once more, saluting from the doorway as the ship drifted slowly into the air. "*Arrivaderci, Capitano!* Give our regards to *Il Duce!*"

Then Jack and Doc were racing to the bridge, and Deadeye was folding in the step.

Doc shook her head. "Oh, he's not gonna like that."

"Almost certainly," Jack replied.

They hurried to their bridge stations, surprising both Cipher and Rivets.

"That was fast," Cipher observed.

Rivets was already unstrapped and showing Jack to his station. "Chair's all yours, Cap."

"Thanks, Rivets. Strap in, everyone. We're getting out of here."

The turbofans were switched to full power. Jack angled them for a vertical climb as fresh lift gas was pumped into the ballonets and the ship began to rise in earnest. There was a surge of electric hum from the engine pods, then a series of *pops* from outside.

Automatic gunfire, followed by single rifle shots.

"Oh no," Doc worried.

Jack's brow furrowed. "I knew they would-n't let us leave without a fight," he said. "Hang on. Swinging around to bring the forward guns to bear." The ship turned in a methodical arc, coming to face the squad of secret police with her twin Lewis guns. Jack gripped the joystick and thumbed the fire-link control, sending a barrage of red tracers and hot lead into the troops, much to their surprise.

The goons scattered, taking cover behind the trucks as the Lewis guns raked the airfield with machine gun fire. One of the trucks took an incendiary tracer round through the radia-tor and ignited the fuel in the leaky engine. A chain of explosions found their way to the gas tanks on each side of the truck and it erupted in shards of metal, glass, bits of wood, and melting India rubber.

Jack throttled to full. "And maximum thrust to get us up and away," he muttered to himself. Then he remembered Terenzi and keyed the *TALK* button on his comms. "Any-body see if that captain made it out alive?"

Deadeye's voice crackled over the radio. "Saw him duck behind the truck."

"The one that I blew up?"

"Negative."

"Terrific," Jack rolled his eyes as the ship continued to ascend over the Italian countryside. "Add another to the list of those who want me dead."

Cipher shook her head, one hand on her earphones. "You really have a way with people, Captain."

"Such a charmer." Doc added.

Jack shrugged. "It's a gift."

Another burst of static hit Jack's headset, followed by Deadeye's voice. "I see movement on the airfield, Cap'n. Going topside to the nest."

"Affirmative."

Cipher nodded. "He's right, sir. They're scrambling fighters to intercept."

"Terrific. If it's not occultist commandos, it's fascist fighter pilots..." Jack began to sweat. That whole interaction had not gone well, and he was kicking himself for running afoul of government officials, corrupt or not— it would mean he couldn't go back to Italy while Mussolini was in power. Not that he wanted to, necessarily. He began to doubt his competence in a job which he'd seemed to be born ready for, but which he'd been drafted into.

Eventually his mind returned to the present situation and he shook off those nagging doubts. The engine thrusters whined with exertion.

"Careful, Cap!" Rivets warned over the radio. "You're red-lining the thruster revs!"

Jack grunted, stabilizing the ship's climb. "Sorry, Rivets, I've gotta get us out of range of those fighters!"

"I can see them," Deadeye broke in. "They're silhouetted by the sunset."

Jack squinted into the evening sky ahead. That meant that Deadeye could still see them for a few minutes, while the *Daedalus* would be a big, dark target against a bigger black sky. They would be harder to hit flying *into* the dark. He found the switch for the running lights on his console and shut them off. That way the enemy fighters wouldn't be able to track their flashing red and green flight beacons.

"Evasive maneuvers," Jack announced. "Deadeye, if you get a shot, take it."

Cipher adjusted the dial on her radio set. "We'll be in range any second."

Jack gripped the throttle and the stick with equal tenacity. His lips moved in a silent prayer to the very ship he commanded. "Come on, baby! Fly!" he hissed under his breath.

The *Daedalus* careened into the night at a hundred miles per hour.

"Here they come!" Deadeye warned in a burst of static, and then the sky ignited in razors of red flame.

- CHAPTER 9 -

Deadeye took aim at the biplane silhouetted in the Hotchkiss gun reticle. Jack could have rattled off what kind of plane it was as if it were important, but Charlie didn't care. It was a hostile target, and it was trying to shoot down his crew. That was enough for him.

A flash of red tracer zoomed precariously close to the clear turret canopy, and he steeled himself. Hitting the trigger of the linked weapons, his arm vibrated with the rapid thrum of incendiary rounds leaving the muzzle. The plane jinked and wobbled slightly above the airship's tail fin, perhaps struggling with the air currents around the *Daedalus* as she climbed.

Deadeye let loose with another burst, leading the target slightly. The *dak-dak-dak-dak* of the Hotchkiss was a steady drum cadence. The glow of white-hot rounds illuminated the forward canopy of the enemy plane for a brief moment before a shower of sparks and fire erupted from the engine. Half of one side of the propeller sheared off and went spinning into the night sky. The enemy aircraft pulled up sharply, stalling at its apex, then fell straight down like a meteor trailing fire.

"Got him!" Deadeye reported on the comms.

Doc's voice greeted him over static. "Nice shooting, Deadeye!"

"Still three more of them," Cipher reminded.

Using his foot pedals, Deadeye spun the turret left and found another target.

"Got a bit of a tailwind now," Jack reported. "Hold 'em off as long as you can, Charlie."

"Aye aye, Cap'n."

Using both hands to guide the linked guns into place, Deadeye took aim as the second plane overtook them from the starboard aft quarter. Another fighter climbed into formation with the primary plane. For a moment, Deadeye shifted attention to the fighter in the rear, and was unprepared as the primary plane screamed past, guns spitting red tracers at the *Daedalus*.

Deadeye opened up with the Hotchkiss, but went uncharacteristically wide. "Missed!"

He centered the targeting reticle on the secondary plane and met its pass with fury.

"Another one comin' in!" he shouted, squeezing the trigger and bracing his hand to steady the weapon.

Dak-dak-dak-dak! The first volley of incendiary rounds perforated the fighter's belly as it approached, and Deadeye tracked it as it passed, opening up a second time.

Dak-dak-dak-dak! The second burst tore open the engine compartment and ripped through the cockpit, blasting the pilot into bloody chunks. The plane banked right and spiraled away into the dark.

"That did it!" he rejoiced over the comms.

Jack came back with a burst of static. "Good shot, Charlie!"

He could hear Doc emit a relieved sigh over the headset, followed by another announcement from Cipher.

"Two fighters left, Captain."

Charlie gathered his bearings and scanned the sunset for any more silhouettes. He found the outline of a plane poking its head up from the dark below the horizon. Keying his *TALK* button, he called down to the bridge. "Cap'n, can you bring her nose up and give me some open sky?"

"You got it," Jack replied, and immediately the ship began to angle higher. This had the effect of opening up the entire dorsal surface of the *Daedalus* for Charlie to use as a potential shooting gallery, so long as the enemy planes came in perpendicular to the airship's ascent.

Deadeye felt his stomach quiver as the sunset horizon dropped below him and the fighter barreled in for its attack.

The plane climbed and then rolled upside down, banking toward the airship's spine as it came in. Its guns blazed, sending a hail of red tracers and lead toward the *Daedalus*. Deadeye noticed out of the corner of his eye the sparks and smoke from the airship's duralumin skin, as it was penetrated with enemy rounds.

He knew they'd been hit, but he also knew their lift gas wasn't combustible like normal hydrogen. He braced and met the incoming attack with twin-linked Hotchkiss fire.

"Come here, you dirty—"

Dak-dak-dak-dak! The volley hit the fighter dead-on, shearing the entire propeller away, pulverizing the windscreen and taking the pilot's head away in pieces. The force of the incendiary rounds knocked the pilot's body back in his seat, pulling the joystick back along with his lifeless hand. This forced the plane into a steep climb, while simultaneously igniting the engine oil coating the surface of the engine compartment. There was a shower of Roman candle sparks, and the plane's engine stalled out. The fighter nosed down, hurtling toward the ground like a broken kite, trailing orange fire.

Charlie watched as the spiraling aircraft exploded when the blaze ignited its fuel supply. Some local farmer would find charred pieces of plane and pilot tomorrow morning, and would have quite the tale to tell the neighbors.

The last plane, which had been keeping its distance for the last few minutes, now banked away and descended toward the airfield.

Charlie keyed his *TALK* button. "Three down, last fighter's breaking off the chase and headin' home."

On the bridge, Jack leveled out the *Daedalus* and throttled down as Doc and Cipher erupted in cheers. He allowed himself a moment for a deep breath before he remembered they'd taken some rounds. He pressed the *TALK* button on his console.

"Good work, Charlie. Rivets, sounds like we took a hit. What's the damage report?"

His query was answered with static.

Jack tried again. "Rivets, damage report."

Static again.

"Rivets!"

Doc unhooked her seat harness, keying her comms. "I'll go. Charlie, meet me in the engine room!" Then she was gone and Jack could hear Deadeye's boots on the gantry ladder. All was silent, save for the whine of electric engines and Jack's own breathing.

The tension was palpable. Rivets had been his kite mechanic in the war. There was no one better at keeping flying things flying, or rolling things rolling, or floating things afloat. The man might have had the exterior of a metal cheese grater, but he had the heart of a Teddy bear. Jack didn't know what he'd do if Rivets were—

No, he thought. *Not until I know for sure.*

Cipher could sense the dark cloud over her captain's head. She wanted desperately to say the right thing, but ironically, this master of codes and communications, with multiple languages at her disposal, could find nothing to assuage his mood.

Finally, after a few uncomfortable minutes, she said, "I'm sure he's fine, sir."

Jack's reply was terse and angrier than he'd intended. "He better be."

☙

Doc found her way aft to the engine room with her medical bag, Deadeye on her heels. She opened the door from the main gantry and found a blinking console and an intermittent shower of sparks from one of the ten Di-Marco-Edison Mark IV reactionless gyroscopic generators. Wired in sequence, the whole lot sat on a perforated aluminum stand at the center of the room. If the lift ballonets were the lungs of the ship, this gyroscopic array was her heart. Each generator stood about 26 inches high, contained in a lightweight aluminum case with a glass dome top, through which the engineer could see the flywheel at work. Exquisitely balanced, each generator provided 100 kilowatts to the power system, and was reset every six to ten hours with a ripcord fed through a door in the side of the case.

The power system was more than just a bunch of perpetual motion generators, however. The generators fed into an array of Edison nickel-iron batteries, which buffered power consumption between generator re-starts, and accepted passive solar energy from the photovoltaic strips woven into the ship's exterior skin. Overseeing it all was a console of electric monitors, gauges and controls.

Slumped at the bottom of this main console was the engineer, bleeding badly from his right thigh.

"Sorry about the damage report," Rivets huffed, still reaching for the radio switch on the console above his head.

Doc rushed to his side and knelt down, dropping her bag by his feet. She pointed it out to Deadeye as he entered. "Charlie, get in here and grab some gauze out of the aid kit here."

"I couldn't reach the radio..." Rivets explained groggily.

Doc was in full field medic mode. "Now Carl, you hush." She motioned to Charlie to swap places with her. "Here, help me get his leg elevated."

Deadeye pulled the boot from Rivets' injured leg and raised his socked foot to rest in his lap. Doc went to work, tearing the pant leg from top to bottom, then ripping open the bullet hole in his long johns to better see the wound. She prodded softly around the exterior, gingerly working her way toward the opening—which made him flinch in agony. She could see something gleaming under the slick of dark blood within, and could feel no exit wound.

The round was clearly still in his leg.

Deadeye saw the puckered breach, oozing blood. He'd seen large caliber injuries like that during the war. "Ooh, nice one, Rivets," he said, sounding both complimentary and a bit jealous of the bragging rights.

Rivets tried to sit up. "How's it look?"

Doc put an instant stop to his movement by pushing him down and sliding a seat cushion under his head. "Well, my dear, you have a nice hole in your leg."

"Yeah?" said Rivets. "What's the good news?"

"The bullet missed your femoral artery."

"And the bad news?"

"It's still in there, and I'm gonna have to remove it.

She loosened the large bandanna from around his neck and tossed it to Deadeye. "Tie this above the wound at the thigh, while I get prepared."

Charlie remembered his Army basic first aid training, fashioning a tidy tourniquet within seconds.

Rivets was in the first stages of wound shock and was already delirious from blood loss. "Smooth talkin' dame," he slurred. "You know just what to say..."

Doc opened the bag completely, unpacking a small aluminum surgical tray and setting it on the floor. Digging through the bag, she located a leather syringe case and a bottle of procaine. She fished the smallest of needles from the leather case, screwed it to the front of the glass syringe, ran her lighter under the needle for a few seconds, then loaded the syringe with procaine. She swabbed Rivets' leg with iodine and tried to find his gaze. "Now Carl, I'm going to give you a little injection to numb the area."

One quick jab of the needle and the procaine seeped into the muscle tissues to begin its work. Rivets was evidently not finished talking.

"Numb away, Doc. Jeez, I wish I had a shot o' whiskey right now."

Doc fumbled through the field surgery kit and found her forceps and a steel probe while Rivets droned on.

"Hey, Deadeye, we're gonna have to check for hull breach. Pretty sure this bullet came from outside..."

"First things first, Rivets," Charlie answered, amused.

"Oh. Yeah. Right. Get in there, Doc. Live music. Floor show. No waitin'."

Doc produced a small flashlight from her bag and flicked it on, approaching the wound with the forceps. "I wish you could have a whiskey too, Rivets. It might shut you up for two minutes. Now hold still."

The probe entered his leg and Rivets winced and growled like a bear in a trap. The bullet, round and intact, was stuck between his femur and a the large thigh muscle. Doc knew if she prolonged this ordeal for any length of time, Rivets could succumb to shock. She'd seen soldiers die from relatively minor, treatable wounds—all from shock. She decided to be aggressive with her extraction, hoping it would take less time.

"Awww, Jiminy Christmas!" Rivets cried out, writhing under Doc's ministrations, but never shifting the position of his leg. "Awww, fer the love of Mary Pickford!"

Doc never deviated from her mission. She handed her flashlight to Deadeye to hold for her as she began to dig away with the forceps.

"Rivets, if you don't hold still, your leg will go septic, and instead of merely digging out a piece of lead, I'll be sawing that leg right off."

Rivets lay back, chastened and quiet. "Yes ma'am. Sorry ma'am."

"That's better," she murmured as the tongs made contact with the lead bullet. "Just a little... there."

Her bloody hand pulled away, and in the clamped jaws of the forceps was that same shiny bit of metal, blunted and barrel-shaped. All told, it had taken less than two minutes to extract.

"I think that's it," said Doc. "No fragments." And she dropped tongs and bullet alike into the tray, immediately returning to the large bottle of iodine.

Now that the procaine had kicked in and Doc had quit poking and prodding around inside his leg, Rivets was suddenly curious. "Can I see it?" he asked, but Doc and Deadeye ignored him.

"Now, while the procaine is still active, I'm going to clean the wound and stitch it up."

"Can...can I see it?"

Doc flushed the wound with the yellow-brown antiseptic, and in a few quick hand motions, threaded a curved suture needle. To Deadeye, it was like watching a great magician do sleight of hand.

"Can I see the bul—oh, nevermind." Rivets sighed, lying his head back and closing his eyes while Doc sewed up his leg as if stitching a dress hem.

"Thanks, Doc, I... *oww*! I really appreciate —oh *jeez*! The help—*augh*!"

"Of course, Rivets," she assured the engineer. "Can't have the best mechanic in the organization hobbling around with a bullet in his leg." Then she was finished, and with a discerning eye surveyed her work. "And... there," she proclaimed, satisfied. "Deadeye, wrap the wound, please."

"Yes, ma'am." Deadeye unrolled the thick cotton gauze he'd been holding onto, encircling Rivets' leg with several layers of bandage as Doc cleaned up the area.

"Been one heck of a day, hasn't it?" Rivets quipped, starting to lose consciousness as the painkiller and trauma got the best of him.

Doc stood, hunched over at Rivets' head. "And now, help me carry him to his quarters."

Deadeye followed her lead, but even between the two of them, carrying the big lug was out of the question. "Well," said Doc, "maybe 'drag' is the operative term."

And with each of them locked under an armpit, Doc and Deadeye managed to negotiate Rivets to his bed.

- CHAPTER 10 -

The moon was in its waning cycle, and for that Jack was thankful. The ship encountered no further threat or obstacle that night, from enemy aircraft to severe weather. Jack found a good air current at just over 5,000 feet and set the throttle to three-quarter speed, letting the tailwind take up the slack. This iteration of *Daedalus* seemed to like three-quarter speed for long-distance cruising. The four smaller thrust engines purred cat-like, RPMs reading optimal, and the subtle vibration almost put Jack to sleep. In fact, for a couple stretches over southern Italy, he set the course and locked the stick, and let himself have a quick nap right there in the pilot's seat, when he wasn't at Doc's station, charting the next leg of the journey.

He desperately needed a break, but the *Daedalus* only had a compliment of five to begin with, and with two hands out of rotation caring for a third, that left the primary pilot and the communications officer. Neither could be spared to spell the other. They needed a sixth crew member, someone who could serve as backup to one or more duty stations and be trained as a relief pilot.

The night was tinged with purple as it prepared for the sun to come up in the eastern sky. The navigation charts put them on the far side of the channel between the Ionian and Adriatic seas, just approaching the island of Corfu.

Doc stepped onto the bridge, and the sound woke Jack from his cat nap.

"How is he?" he asked.

Doc wandered down to the pilot's seat, enfolding her arms over Jack and nuzzling her face into the back of his neck. Inhaling the familiar scent which had grown muskier over the past three days, she noted the boy needed a bath.

"Passed out in his bunk," she answered. "Wound's stable, though I wouldn't mind having him checked out in a proper hospital."

Jack leaned his head back, reciprocating her affectionate touch without being obvious, nor letting his vision wander from his console and the segmented windscreen before him. "Well, we're only about three hours out from Athens," he said, implying the existence of "proper hospitals" in the city.

Doc winced. "He's not going to want to leave the ship."

"He doesn't have much of a choice," said Jack. "I'll even knock him out for you."

Cipher could see the couple sharing their quiet moment, and she hated to break in, but there were pressing ship matters to address. She cleared her throat as delicately as possible.

"Did Commander Holloway give a damage report?"

Doc snapped out of her languor and stood upright, producing a folded sheet of paper from her pocket. "He and Deadeye managed to cobble together a quick overview before he conked out."

She handed the paper to Jack, and he unfolded and scanned it with eager eyes.

"Hmm. Enemy rounds penetrated the outer envelope and the gondola hull. One generator down, he's got it bypassed to the other nine. We had a small breach in ballonet three, but Deadeye got it patched." Jack seemed satisfied, handing the paper back to Doc. "All things considered..."

Cipher couldn't believe they'd fared so well against four Italian fighter planes—and two battles with six Silver Star aircraft before that! "All things considered, indeed. Are you always this lucky?"

Jack chuckled. "Cheat the odds as long as we have, you'll come to understand there's no such thing as luck. Just ten percent skill, ten percent destiny and eighty percent perseverance."

Doc smiled, adding, "Or a blind spot where mortal danger is concerned."

"That's what I just said," laughed Jack. "Anyway, after experiencing the human meatgrinder that was the Great War, nothing scares me."

Cipher's eyes widened. She hadn't experienced the battlefields of the World War, but she'd researched what they were up against in the form of the Astrum Argentum. "Not even the dark forces at Crowley's command?"

Jack caught himself laughing at the question and settled down before he answered. "Now, the *people* at his command are just people. I understand them—they hold no fear for me." He shifted in his seat and thought for a moment. "The *occult* portion, I *don't* understand, so I don't fear it, either. Doc tells me when to run away, and so far it's worked for us."

It dawned on Cipher that she'd truly run away to join the circus, for better or worse. "Alright," she laughed. "I'll keep that in mind."

Doc went to the nav station and began reviewing the charts. "Cipher, check the most recent *AEGIS Field Manual*. Who is our contact in Athens?"

Cipher pulled a small, light blue handbook from its cubby next to the radio detector and began flipping through its pages. "Looks like a Ms. Marina Stavros, based out of Piraeus. Mid-forties, businesswoman, war widow, staunch anti-fascist..."

Jack frowned. "Nice change from our reception in Rome."

"Well if she's in the roster," Doc explained, trying to rekindle trust in the organization funding their expedition, "she's been cleared by AEGIS Command and probably knows Edison personally."

"That's good enough for me," Jack assured her.

He knew where they'd gone wrong in Rome. The stop in Italy had been too credulous and ill-planned. They should have screened potential field contacts and had an entry and exit strategy, aside from shooting their way out of being jailed by fascist secret police. That lack of planning had put the ship and its crew in peril, and he vowed silently never to go into such a situation again without a plan. Sure, he was good at improvising; he just didn't want to rely on that talent quite so much.

He was also worried about Duke. He didn't know if they were twelve, sixteen, eighteen hours behind the *Percival*, or more.

Doc was still talking about their Athens contact, Marina Stavros. "Let's just hope she's got some information for us."

"Amen, sister," said Jack, gritting his teeth. "Just hang in there, Duke."

☙

The sun welcomed the *Daedalus* as the airship made its final approach across the Gulf of Elefsina. Warm and golden, it seemed to embrace the entire Aegean Sea.

Jack brought the ship down and made a wide sweep over the ancient, bustling city of Athens. Southwest over the city center, the Parthenon, temple to the goddess Athena, stood vigil from atop the Acropolis—its facade gleaming from behind a grid of scaffolds, in a perpetual state of restoration for the past two years.

The city was nestled in a bowl-like valley at one end of the Saronic Gulf, the ancient capital of an ancient people—a people who had suffered greatly under many waves of Ottoman invasion, and most recently as pawns of the larger empires in the Great War. Tenements of limestone and terracotta spread from its center like tendrils of a spiderweb, shiny metal water cisterns gleaming from every rooftop. Legions of workers toiled in the morning heat, sweeping garbage or assembling the massive construction lattices used for the myriad building and renovation projects throughout the area.

Greece was home to more than six million people, and a good portion of them lived or worked in the capital. There were at least a million bicycles, in addition to the ever-present competition between horse-drawn carriage and sputtering motorcar. A legion of speculators and foreign investors staked claims here as well, modern carpetbaggers looking to make a *lire* or two off a nation in transition.

The city's air quality was entirely dependent upon the prevailing air currents. It could become stagnant and choking during the hot summer months, leaving the valley in a thick brown haze, or, when the winds blew down from the mountains and out to sea, it could be a Mediterranean paradise. As the *Daedalus* made its circle above the city, it seemed the gods of old had blessed their arrival: the winds were indeed blowing, and the sky was clear.

Jack banked the ship and headed southwest, toward the satellite town of Piraeus and its naturally-protected harbor. The ports of Greece were among the busiest in the Mediterranean, teeming with commercial shipping and civilian immigration, and Piraeus Harbor was the largest and most strategically-important. Regardless, the harbor master had promised sufficient space to tie down at their destination.

Stavros Import & Export Limited was a large warehouse compound with hundreds of linear feet in dock facilities, mostly occupied by cargo freighters from Italy, Palestine, and various ports in North Africa. A small group of dock workers rushed out to help with the landing and tie-down, greeting the legendary airship and her celebrity crew with gusto.

Jack powered down the engines and let the ground crew cleat the landing cables to an open section of tarmac. He then led the crew ashore.

"Okay, everyone," he said, hopping down from the port side gondola door and scanning the docks. "Stick together and keep your eyes open. We're in friendly but unfamiliar territory."

Two of the ground crew offered Doc a hand as she descended the folding step, followed by Cipher.

"*Efcharistó*," Doc said. "Thank you, fellas."

"*Parakaló*," came the answer from multiple workers as they wandered around the ship's envelope, pointing and chatting away in Greek.

Cipher put a hand up to shield her eyes from glare. "The harbor master said Ms. Stavros was coming to meet us."

Deadeye followed her lead, pointing toward a small dust cloud rolling down a long road toward the compound. "There's a car comin'."

Gates opened and workers scrambled to and fro as the car approached, a rich ceramic blue with chrome and white accents. The rag top was down, and Jack could see a middle-aged couple in the rear seat, driven by a uniformed chauffeur.

"Nice new Packard," he said. "Bet that's her."

He was right, as far as the car went. It was a spanking new Packard Sport Phaeton, well-appointed and immaculate—luxury and power personified. Its eight cylinders purred under the chrome bonnet until the driver applied the brakes and cut the engine. Jack estimated its price tag at a thousand bucks American, possibly more.

The chauffeur, a short, round Armenian with a silver mustache, hurried around to open the rear door for his employer, but Marina Stavros had already opened it rushed to greet the crew. A suntanned brunette with amber-brown eyes and a curvaceous-yet-compact frame, the distinguished creases around her eyes and mouth that told of a life filled with the highs and lows of human experience. Marina projected the air of a middle-class woman who'd married into money, yet retained her compassion for the workers upon whose backs Greece was currently being rebuilt.

Glamorous in a white cotton pants suit, wide-brimmed sun hat, beaded bracelet on one wrist, a silver Elgin watch on the other, an emerald pendant on a silver chain gleamed below her neck. Round sunglasses covered her eyes, as her full lips parted in a toothy, white smile.

Jack bent at the waist in an all-purpose diplomatic bow. "Ms. Stavros, I presume?"

"By the saints! I cannot believe it! Such a privilege to welcome the crew of the *Daedalus* home to Greece!" Her impressive English was thick with the guttural Greek accent. Stavros threw her arms wide, greeting each crew member with a hug and kiss on the cheek.

Cipher accepted the greeting but frowned in confusion. "Home?"

"Daedalus is a character from ancient Greek myth," Doc clarified. "He was the father of Icarus, a renowned inventor and the designer of the great labyrinth on Crete."

"Where the Minotaur was kept?" Cipher asked.

Doc nodded. "Exactly."

Not wanting to be left out, Jack added. "And he was the first successful aviator."

"According to legend." Doc clarified.

Marina took in the sight of the crew, assembled in the bullet-shaped shadow of the remarkable airship. "You must be tired after your long journey. And your wounded crew mate..." She turned and waved her erstwhile companion forward, a gray-haired man of sixty-odd years carrying a medical satchel. "My personal physician will attend him on board." As the old man shook hands with the crew, Stavros added, "Doctor Floros. *Pigaínete grígora.*"

"*Nai kyría mou,*" the doctor answered, heading to the aluminum folding step and accepting Deadeye's guiding hand as he climbed aboard.

Marina removed her sunglasses and looked Jack over as though appraising a classical statue. "I hope you will honor me by being my guests for the night?"

"Thank you, Ms. Stavros," said Doc, moving a little closer to Jack without realizing it.

Jack smiled, a bit nervous at the attention. "Thank you very much indeed," he said. "We'd be happy to recuperate for the evening, but we're trying to make up as much time as possible."

Marina nodded. "I understand, Captain. Do let me offer you some food and a bath, at the very least?"

"We gladly accept," Doc smiled. As much as she loved Jack's scent, being in close quarters with three sweaty men was beginning to wear on her. She needed a break.

Cipher signaled for Jack's attention. "Captain, someone should stay behind with the ship, and to keep an eye on Commander Holloway."

Jack nodded. "You're right, of course, Cipher. You and Deadeye take first watch at the ship. We'll be back in a couple hours."

Deadeye saluted with a couple fingers from a non-existent hat. "Sounds good."

"Affirmative," Cipher agreed.

As Cipher and Deadeye climbed back aboard the airship, Marina smiled again at Jack and Doc. "Come," she said. "We'll take my car. My home is nearby. Meanwhile, my workers will load some more provisions and fresh water on your ship."

Jack bowed again and followed her to the Packard parked nearby. "Thank you, Ms. Stavros."

As they wandered to the car, Marina snapped her fingers and pointed at various workers. "*Trofí kai neró! Tóra!*"

The chauffeur made a circuit around the car, shutting the rear doors and climbing into the driver's seat, revving the Phaeton to life. In less than a minute, the car was whisking them away from the port compound and into the city.

- CHAPTER 11 -

The Black Dog glanced up from his coffee as Maria Blutig strode onto the bridge of the *Osiris*. The operational brain of the supercarrier was twice the size of the *Luftpanzer*'s bridge, with two helmsmen grasping giant steering wheels, and stations for navigation, radio, flight control and weapons. Captain Hummel sat at a planning table, charts spread out before him, much like Crowley had looked at the fortress in Romania. Back aboard ship, Maria now dressed in the crisp, black uniform of the Silver Star officer, her peaked officer's cap of black and red displaying a silver four-pointed star emblem in front. A 9mm Mauser was holstered at her side, a riding crop tucked under her arm.

"Anything?" Hummel asked as Maria approached, setting the crop on the table and removing her cap.

"No," Maria sighed, clearly agitated. "No intelligence. I put my top interrogators on it, but Commander Willis and his crew are well-conditioned to withstand torture. They have given us nothing."

Hummel pursed his lips, examining the charts splayed out before him. "Too bad," he said. "I thought if anyone could break them it would be the She-Wolf of the Silver Star."

Maria threw Hummel a dirty look, barely contained anger flashing on her angular features. Gritting her teeth, she forced herself to breathe, gradually relaxing. It would do no good to fight with the Black Dog; he had delivered the *Percival* and its crew, after all. She knew better than to look a gift horse in the mouth. But if she wasn't able to get any useful information out of the prisoners, what value was she actually bringing to the operation?

Hummel shrugged. "But at least we have their ship, and their dynamo for examination." Each comment was a less-than-subtle jab.

Maria frowned, and then her face lit up in an epiphany. "If they will not give us intelligence," she hissed, "they will join the service of our master. And if they will not join us..." Maria replaced her cap and peered at Hummel through dark blue eyes. "Their blood will open a gateway for a summoning. One which even Crowley was unable to complete, back in the Amazon." Her eyes alight, Maria plucked the riding crop from the table and swished it through the air aggressively. "If I could deliver the service of Ammit unto our master, would that not be a thing of value?"

"Ammit, the Soul-Eater?" The Black Dog smirked halfheartedly. He was a military man, not one of Crowley's obsessed mystics who droned on and on about opening dimensional rifts and summoning demons to serve the cause. In his experience, demons didn't like being summoned, and very few could actually be controlled. The summoner really had to know his or her stuff, and even then, success was never guaranteed.

Maria dismissed his incredulity. "Yes. The Devourer of the Dead. A demon known to the ancients of Egypt."

Hummel gave a tired sigh. "What's your plan?"

"Radio headquarters and advise them we will put down at Naqada. We will offload the prisoners and I will perform the ritual in the main temple of Set."

Hummel stood from his chair and leaned forward on the table, staring Maria down. "I will agree to a stop at Naqada, so long as the

Osiris and her resources are not required to stay for the duration." He took a sip of his coffee, never looking away from her. "I have their dynamo to deliver, and I have no intention of staying any longer than necessary."

"Since we are keeping their crew aboard the *Percival* under guard," Maria offered, "we could offload the airship itself, and you could be on your way."

"I do not believe in half measures, Maria. The *Osiris* will land and help you secure the area, and wait until the ritual is well underway before departure." The Black Dog smiled a predatory smile. "It is in my best interest to play a role in your success, but I, too, must deliver my prize and move back into the Master's good graces."

Maria smiled back at him in the same manner. "Agreed. Have we any word of the *Daedalus*?"

Hummel shook his head. "Not much. Our contacts in the Italian government say they shot their way out of Rome and are probably headed to Athens. I've ordered our field operatives there to investigate."

"They are tenacious, *mein Kapitän*," Maria warned. "I expect they may eventually find us, which is why we should throw every obstacle we can into their path."

"Return to the *Luftpanzer*," Hummel ordered. "Inform Captain Ecke of the plan. Meanwhile I will contact some of our friends in Cairo and the surrounding region for help on the ground."

"There are cults of Set and Osiris active in and around Cairo," said Maria. "You should not have trouble finding—"

"Goodbye, Maria," Hummel smiled patronizingly, returning his attention to the maps on the table and the cup of coffee in his hand.

"*Mein Kapitän*," Maria nodded, tucked the riding crop under her arm and turned on her heel to leave.

☙

The small driver navigated carefully through the streets of Piraeus, showing Jack and Doc a neighborhood brimming with art, commerce, and national pride. White stucco walls were plastered with posters of President Pavlos Kountouriotis, a somewhat tired-looking old man in a dapper suit, whose long mustache appeared as though trying to leap from his upper lip. A military hero several times over, Kountouriotis had been selected democratically to lead the Second Hellenic Republic.

As they made their way southeast along the waterfront and across the Piraeus peninsula to the hillside opposite Port Munychie, dwellings became fewer and farther between, yet individually larger. This was where wealthy Athenians lived if they didn't have a home in the city proper. Here among the ruined Themistoclean Walls on the hill of Kastella jutted the cliffside villas of mercantile giants, politicians and dignitaries, as well as the organized criminal element.

The Packard pulled into a round driveway lined with pointed cypress trees and a classical fountain at its hub, coming to a stop in front of a main entry guarded by a pair of oak doors and a slender, dark-haired man in white cotton livery.

Doc figured the man was Stavros' butler or some other trusted subordinate, and she took special notice of his limp as he approached to greet them. The driver exited the car and ran around to open the passenger doors, but once again Stavros was well ahead of him. She helped Doc out of the back, and introduced her guests.

"Captain McGraw and Doctor Starr," she gestured. "This is Fotios, my butler."

They nodded at one another, and Marina rattled off some instructions to him in Greek, but Jack and Doc were already gravitating toward the enormous villa.

The mansion was a concrete and stucco bunker. The temperature was probably twenty degrees colder inside, and Jack was suddenly conscious of the rapidly-cooling beads of sweat rolling down his back.

"Oh my!" Doc muttered as they walked in.

Jack shook his head in disbelief. "You weren't kidding, Ms. Stavros." The floorplan was open, furnishings sparse, with multiple floors supported by thick round columns. Classical reliefs and statuary peered out from their wall mounts, while armchairs of oak and leather sat in various places and groupings around the massive great room. A set of French doors, set off by buff-colored linen draperies, opened onto a balcony overlooking the Saronic Gulf and the Mirtoan Sea beyond. The doors had been left wide to the breeze, and Jack and Doc could smell the salt air waft in from the water.

"What a lovely home," Doc fawned.

Jack nodded in solid agreement. "And that view ain't bad either."

Marina smiled as she handed her hat and glasses to Fotios, who limped out of the room. "It's far too large for myself, as my son is away at university and my late husband was one of many Greek casualties of Ottoman aggression during the war."

Doc bowed her head and had to look away. "That's tragic. I'm so sorry."

Marina Stavros smiled and powered through, as per usual. "Aside from his collection of motorcars, this home is the one extravagance I allow myself," she explained. "I dedicate the rest of my business interests and fortune toward the causes of peace and equity, after the horrors unleashed upon the world in the last decade."

Fotios returned with a large platter of sliced fruit, olives, and goat cheese, which Marina directed be placed on a heavy oak table in the center of the room. As the butler once again limped away, Stavros added, "My workers are well paid and very loyal, so my harbor compound works nicely for AEGIS as a way station and gateway to the Mediterranean."

Jack thrust his thumbs into his belt. "Sure beats the reception we got in Italy."

"The political situation in Italy is shameful," Stavros frowned. "But onto the mission at hand."

"Indeed," said Jack, nodding.

"I was troubled to hear of the disappearance of Commander Willis," said Marina. "We began to worry when the *Percival* did not arrive yesterday as planned."

"So they never arrived at all?" Doc asked.

Marina shook her head no.

Jack began to pace the stone floor. "That's what we've been afraid of. Duke would never let the *Percival* be boarded, so either they were shot down..."

"Somewhere between London and Cairo," Doc added.

"Or they were taken during a landing somewhere," said Jack.

Marina paused in thought. "You say his destination was Cairo?"

As he wandered the floor, Jack caught sight of the fruit and cheese, suddenly realizing he hadn't eaten since the previous night.

"Yes," Doc answered. "Apparently it was to be a bit more than a shakedown cruise, but Duke was...non-specific...when he talked to us."

Marina noticed Jack staring at the spread before him. "Please, help yourself to the food."

"Thank you," said Jack as he grabbed a handful of apple slices, shelled walnuts and an apricot from the tray.

"Who do you think might be behind the disappearance?" Stavros inquired, pouring some sweet red wine into three glasses.

Doc folded her arms across her chest. "We've had agents of the Silver Star on our tail from the get-go."

Marina took a glass to each of them, then went to a small desk in the corner, upon which stood a 20-year-old wind-up Victrola. She cranked up the handle a few times, then flipped the arm down on an Annette Hanshaw record released the previous year. The lilting strains of Hanshaw's lilting piano and sultry alto voice drifted from the speaker cone in the form of "Falling in Love with You".

Jack's mouth was full of apple slices, but he didn't want to be left out of the discussion. "If not the Silver Star," he mumbled, "I wouldn't know where to start looking." He also realized he would have to tell Deadeye about this record—Charlie was nuts about Hanshaw.

Marina Stavros pursed her lips and ran a manicured hand through her mane of naturally curly dark hair, which was just starting to frost with silver. It hung at her shoulders, too long for a bob. Jack could smell honeysuckle and rose hips as she walked past him to a steamer trunk being used as a side table for one of the armchairs. "If this is the battle I've feared coming," she said, opening the trunk, "then I have something for you." She removed a 14-by-6-inch cedar box and turned to hold it out toward Doc. Jack immediately noticed the lodestone around Doc's neck begin to glow with its unearthly blue-white light, ringing with its mystical hum.

"Doc," said Jack, pointing. "The lodestone. Look."

Doc glanced down to see the stone light up. She looked at Jack, then back at the box Stavros was offering.

"My husband retrieved this on a dig in Epidavros," Marina explained, opening the lid to reveal an armored cuff of some kind: bronze, with a blue-green patina. Smallish, it was inscribed in Greek.

"Is that bronze?" asked Jack. "It looks like a vambrace, a piece of armor for the lower arm."

"But smaller," Doc added. "As if it were made especially for—"

"A woman?" Stavros finished. "Yes. An obscure sect of warrior priestesses of Athena Parthenos. It is said to be imbued with mystical powers of protection."

Jack was intrigued. "Doc's lodestone glows in proximity to magical energy, so I'd tend to agree."

"Athena Parthenos?" Doc wondered. "That's Athena in her warrior form."

Marina smiled. "Someone knows her classical mythology."

"It's beautiful," Doc was finally able to form the words.

"Take it," Marina urged. "Use it in your battle against the forces of darkness."

Doc swallowed hard. "I couldn't."

Marina placed Doc's the cedar box in Doc's hands, pleading, "Take it. Please. With my blessing. We need every advantage if we are to prevail."

Doc looked back at Jack for input, but she already knew she should take the artifact. It was of better use to AEGIS if it were out of the Silver Star's hands. Finally she accepted the box from Marina. "In that case, we'll gladly accept the gift. If you will accept our thanks, and our promise that it will be used for the good of all mankind."

Marina smiled, a tear coming to her eye. "That is all the payment I require."

Jack spied a shadowy movement on the balcony, and his mind and body slipped into gear. "Say, Ms. Stavros," he said, moving closer to be able to speak in a hushed tone. "That wouldn't be one of your staff outside on the balcony, would it?"

Marina glanced out the open French doors but saw nothing. "What? No, my butler Fotios lives here on the premises, and my driver Armen is waiting to take you back to the harbor, but the rest of my house staff have been released for the day."

"That's what I was afraid of," said Jack as he pulled the twin Colts from their respective holsters, cocking them both with his thumbs.

Marina Stavros suddenly realized how dangerous the situation had become, and what a predicament her guests were in. "You must leave now," she said ominously.

"We can't just leave you to the mercy of Silver Star agents," Doc protested as she slipped the ancient vambrace into her satchel.

Marina went back to the desk with the Victrola on it, flipped the needle from the record and opened the top desk drawer, producing a small automatic pistol. "Ah, Dr. Starr, I did not rise to my current station in life by being helpless."

Jack was impressed. "Nice little Mauser."

"It gets the job done," Stavros winked.

The room suddenly erupted in a tempest of plaster, glass, and bullets.

- CHAPTER 12 -

"Get down!" Doc screamed, dropping prone.

Jack was in the air instantly, diving to the floor while simultaneously kicking over the heavy table. "Over here! Behind the table!" He flipped around, firing two shots out the open French doors, creating an opportunity for Doc and Marina to crawl behind the cover of the oak obstacle.

Another burst of automatic gunfire blazed into the room, leaving a trail of holes that snaked along the back wall. Doc pulled her Colt revolver from her satchel and fired a shot from the left side of the table. Marina fired two shots with her Mauser. It was silent for a moment, and the three looked at each other behind the overturned table.

Suddenly, Fotios the butler appeared in the hall at the back of the room, clutching a pump-action shotgun and wondering who was trying to kill his employer. "*Mantám? Ti symvaínei?*"

Marina caught his eye and waved him over to one of the vertical columns on the other side of the room. "Foti. *Sto balkóni.*"

"*Nai mantám,*" he agreed, taking up a position to create a crossfire in case one or more attackers decided to enter through the French doors. He racked the Browning shotgun and fired a blast toward the balcony as the Armenian driver entered through the front door.

Marina saw him and waved him back. "Armen, *óchi! Ela píso!*"

"What I wouldn't give for a radio right now..." Jack fired twice over the top of the table and dropped back down.

"Follow the corridor behind us to the last door," Marina instructed. "It will take you into the garage. Take one of the vehicles and get back to your ship."

Doc's eyes pleaded with Marina. "But—"

"Do not argue, my dear. Hurry! Fotios and I will try to keep them occupied here."

Another volley erupted through the French doors, shredding the upholstery from chairs and pulverizing a priceless Classical urn.

"Come on, Doc," said Jack, nodding toward the hall. "We've got a mission to finish!"

Doc reached out and found Marina's hand. She squeezed it firmly. "We are in your debt, Ms. Stavros."

"Find the *Percival*," said Marina.

Jack nudged Doc toward the hallway at a crouched run, turning to fire behind him as they bolted. They passed the chauffeur again. He was returning from deep within the residence, gripping a battle-worn Mosin–Nagant carbine. That told Jack a lot about this Armenian man and his history. The driver nodded in salute as they passed in the hallway, then Jack and Doc were gone, Armen joining the firefight in the great room.

Doc gripped her satchel and slung it over her left shoulder, now following Jack as he blazed the trail. Boots echoed off stone floors and stucco walls, and Jack kept looking back to make sure he hadn't lost his partner.

"Doc, come on! This way!"

"Don't wait for me!"

"Last door," Jack pondered aloud, coming to the end of the passage. "Last door."

"Here!" Doc cried, lifting a wrought-iron handle and flinging open another heavy oak door.

"Holy—!" Jack trailed off, eyes wide.

They found themselves in a room more resembling a flight hangar than a garage. Twelve or more cars of various makes and models, each a masterpiece, stood proudly at their stations. A fire engine red 1925 Alfa Romeo RL Turismo was parked next to a black 1924 Isotta Fraschini 8-cylinder sedan with red crushed velvet interior. In the next stall sat a snow-white 1921 Benz Cabriolet. For a gearhead like Jack McGraw, it was sensory overload. He almost caught himself drooling as he muscled one of the barn doors open to the road outside. He peered around the door to check the driveway and saw that it was clear, then he gave the assortment of vehicles another look as if he were a child in a sweet shop deciding on a single flavor.

"Did she say *any* vehicle?"

"There must be a dozen cars in here!" Doc exclaimed, scratching her head.

Then Jack saw it, and he knew which chariot would carry them on their escape. "And you're gonna hate me for it," he said, "but this is what we have to take."

In the stall nearest the exterior garage door was a familiar sight. He'd "borrowed" a similar machine from J. Elling Ponderby just last year in pursuit of Silver Star agents who had assassinated him in the pursuit of his lift gas formula. It was sleek and light, with its trademark teardrop gas tank, and thick, knobby tires. Painted olive drab with red accents, it was—

"A motorcycle?" Doc mused.

Jack grinned. "A Harley-Davidson JD Twin."

Doc thrust a hip to one side, planting her fist on it in protest. She remembered fleeing aerial bombardment in the Bahamas in the aluminum and canvas sidecar of the electric Dugdale cycle the *Daedalus* carried for short land excursions, but this didn't even have the dubious luxury of a sidecar. "There's no way."

"It's faster in these narrow streets than anything on four wheels," Jack negotiated.

Doc rolled her eyes. Clearly he wasn't thinking rationally. "No, I mean there's *physically* no way—"

But Jack was already astride, leaning the vehicle off its kickstand. "Hop on, Doc."

"Where, exactly?"

Jack stomped on the starter and the twin cylinders sputtered to life. "On my lap, facing backward," he explained. "Take one of my .45s in each hand. You can see over my shoulder and cover us from the rear, and if we get hit, it has to go through me to get you."

Doc's mind raced. "If we had more time, I'm sure that would have sounded incredibly chivalrous and romantic."

"Yeah, well, we don't have time, so hop aboard."

Doc secured her satchel with the strap across her body and flung her leg over Jack's lap. "We're gonna discuss this later," she warned.

"I don't doubt it." Jack had left his flight cap back on the *Daedalus*, but his goggles were an ever-present feature around his neck. He pulled them up over his eyes and walked the bike out the garage door, Doc facing him in an embrace which probably should have been more awkward than it was. "Hang on."

India rubber tires squealed on stone and concrete as Jack maneuvered the motorcycle up the cobbled road of Kastella hill. Shifting down, he took the first detour he could find along one of the dozens of small alleys making up the neighborhood grid of Piraeus. They were on the opposite side of the peninsula from the Stavros harbor compound, and had a lot of criss-crossing alleys to cover.

"Keep an eye behind us, Doc! I'll get to the harbor as fast as I can!"

As if on cue, Doc caught a flurry of motion from the block behind them, and a black Victoria motorcycle appeared on their tail.

"Jack!" she warned. "Another motorcycle just appeared from that alley!"

Jack heard her. He twisted the throttle and shifted higher, careening through a zig-zag of cobblestone alleys, between canyons of stucco houses, under banners of hanging laundry.

Gunfire erupted behind them—one round ricocheted off an iron door hinge and embedded in a window sill across the alley. Another round shattered a wooden cage housing a lone chicken, which panicked and flew into the path of the shooter, bounced off the front fork of the bike and spun around to land on the banister of an alley stoop, bewildered but alive.

Tires screeched as Jack narrowly avoided the splintered debris of the tiny crate.

"They're shooting at us!" Doc observed.

"Well, shoot back!"

Doc felt her wrists ache as she fired one .45 and then the other. She wasn't surprised when both shots went wide.

Jack took a hard left and sped across an open street before finding relief in the alley opposite. They'd made the crest of Piraeus—only downhill from here to the harbor. Jack saw the spilled delivery crates almost too late. "Hang on!" He grabbed the brake with his left hand and swerved aggressively to the side. He halfway expected to crash, but Doc moved with him by instinct, perfectly matching his shifting weight.

"Nice balance, Doc!" he complimented. He heard a shot ring out and suddenly felt his left shoulder burst open. He grunted with the pain, setting his jaw against the distraction.

"You're hit?" Doc worried.

"Yeah," he grunted. "Left shoulder."

Teeth clenched, Jack wanted so badly to yell at the top of his lungs, but laid out before him was a slalom of stacked wooden crates and scrap lumber, and a pursuer on a racing cycle with a gun.

They leaned side to side in unison as the obstacles flew by. Doc emptied the twin Colts at the motorcycle rider behind them, punctuating her verbal tirade.

"Cant...go a...year...without...digging...bullets...out of you!"

Jack understood her frustration, but damn it, this was the life and career they chose. "The *plan* was to eat nice food and get a warm *bath!*" he protested. "The *plan* was not to get shot up on a motorcycle in the back alleys of Greece!"

There was another blur of movement on the roof of the tenement behind them, and Doc swallowed dryly. "Jack! On the rooftop!"

Jack hated the fact the Silver Star seemed to have tendrils of influence even in friendly AEGIS territory. Reaching for the worst possible scenario to lace with sarcasm, he shouted at Doc as they swerved past another stack of crates. "Let me guess—anti-tank gun!"

"Yep!" was all Doc had time to say before the agent on the roof took aim with a Mauser T-Gewehr rifle on a small bipod, and fired.

A huge chunk of stucco and concrete exploded from the building to their right, peppering the fleeing heroes with debris.

"*I was kidding!*" Jack railed.

"*You should know better!*" Doc replied, clutching him tightly around the waist.

"This day just gets better and better!" he mused with a bit more-than-slightly-crazed look. "Oh no, spoke to soon."

Unable to see behind her, Doc breathed heavily, rising panic in her voice. "What!"

Ahead of them was an open-bed delivery truck, offloading wooden kegs to the back entrance of a local tavern. A hirsute Greek in a cap and sweat-stained undershirt stood next to the cab, having a smoke. To the right of the truck was a tenement stairway, and it gave Jack an idea.

"Truck in the way! Gonna try to jump it using the stairway on the right!"

Before she could protest, Jack had already yelled, "Hang on!" and hauled back on the handlebars to get the front fork onto the concrete stairs. He gave it full throttle, and the bike ascended with a stuttered roar.

- CHAPTER 13 -

The truck driver saw them, panicked, and dropped his smoke in the alley as he dove for the ground. A final shot from the mounted pursuer's pistol exploded a keg in the bed of the truck, spraying beer everywhere. Another shot from the T-Gewehr on the rooftop pierced the truck's external gas tank, which was ignited either by the incendiary bullet or the driver's falling cigarette.

The truck exploded in a fireball of metal panels and wooden barrel fragments, the concussion flinging the driver against the far alley wall where he lay dazed.

The Harley-Davidson soared over the exploding truck, Doc clinging to Jack with every ounce of strength she could muster. The suspension bottomed out as it landed, sending sparks in a rooster tail as the spring shocks groaned under the strain. The front wheel angled sharply to the right, almost pulling them over. Jack compensated, wincing with every movement of his wounded shoulder. Doc could feel the blood running down his shirt and over her hand.

"Unh! Made it!" Jack declared, speeding down a steep incline to meet another alley that was a straight shot down to the Stavros compound gate. Just a few more minutes and they'd be back at the harbor.

"Better condition than that truck!" Doc had to admit.

"We're almost back to the Stavros harbor compound. I can see the *Daedalus*."

"I just see a smoldering truck," said Doc. "And you're bleeding like mad."

"I'll be fine. Just keep an eye out for that anti-tank gun. We don't need to test out our ship's hull rating today."

"Jack, do you think Ms. Stavros and her butler and driver will be okay on their own? They don't have experience fighting the Silver Star like we do."

"They're not on their own."

"What do you mean?"

A dock worker saw the approaching motorcycle a hundred yards away and opened the gate to the compound.

"I mean, I intend to get the *Daedalus* in the air and make short work of the agents attacking her home. We don't leave field contacts in the lurch."

Doc hugged him tightly. "I approve."

A crowd of dock hands gathered as the motorcycle approached, skidding to a halt near the tie-down spot. Doc jumped off first, helping Jack as he handed the bike over to a lanky foreman with a gray beard who recognized it as belonging to Stavros.

"Ms. Stavros is in danger," Jack warned the foreman. "Call the local authorities to her home." He pointed out the iron cleats in the concrete. "And cast off those lines! We're taking off!"

The crowd of dock workers became a frenzy of motion. Lines were undone as Jack and Doc ran for the step and climbed aboard the airship. The bearded foreman revved the motorcycle and rode off toward the main office at the other end of the compound.

"Come on, Doc! There's no time to lose!"

"Right behind you, Jack!"

As they found their way into the main saloon, Jack pointed toward the rear of the ship.

"Get aft and see to Rivets and the doctor. I'll get the engines started up."

"Right," Doc nodded, setting off down the corridor.

Jack strode quickly onto the bridge, surprising Cipher at the comms station. "Cipher, prepare for takeoff."

Cipher looked up and saw a cascade of blood streaked down Jack's shoulder and back. "Captain! Your shoulder!"

Jack hooked his right arm through the safety harness and flipped on the power switches to the engines. "Don't worry, Lieutenant. If we're lucky, this trip won't take very long and Doc can patch me up later." He keyed the *TALK* button on the console. "Captain to crew, prepare for emergency liftoff!"

Deadeye answered immediately over the radio. "Welcome back, Cap'n. I assume we're skipping dinner and bath time?"

"We're doing no such thing. Just a short detour. Get to the starboard side door and see if you can take out any enemy targets."

"Aye aye, Cap. Which would those be?"

"We didn't get a look at them before we had to scram, but presume Silver Star. Maybe agents, maybe regular soldiers. They'll be the ones firing *into* the house.

"Affirmative."

Doc appeared in the bridge hatch, making her way to the nav station. "The doctor already disembarked. Rivets is fine. I just hope you won't need him in the engine room."

"Very good," Jack nodded as he throttled full speed over the rooftops of Piraeus. They were a scant minute away by air—it was a single mile as the crow flies to the southern cliffside overlook of the Stavros estate. He was eagerly anticipating trying out the fire linkage in the forward guns during daylight, when he'd actually be able to see a target.

Jack came in high on a southeastern heading, dropping down over the cliff between the Stavros mansion and the tiny island of Stalida, just 200 feet due south. He reversed throttle and swung the airship's nose around to the reverse of their initial approach, facing northwest, parallel with the coastline.

Doc stepped down to look over Jack's shoulder as they dropped, pointing through the airship's windscreen panels toward the balcony of the home. "Jack, down there! There are still...two, three...at least four agents on the balcony!"

Sure enough, there were Silver Star troops in defensive positions along the balcony: two behind an iron planter, one behind a large bronze amphora, and the fourth squatting behind a folded oak chaise lounge. All wore the gray tropical fatigues of the Astrum Argentum, with the black peaked caps displaying the Silver four-pointed star insignia on the front. Each wielded some kind of submachine gun, emptying burst after burst into the house through the shattered French doors.

"At least we know Stavros and her men are still fighting, or those commandos would be inside by now," Jack postulated as he hit the *TALK* button on his control console. "Deadeye, I'm lining up to fire parallel with the balcony and minimize damage to the house."

"Affirmative."

Jack edged the ship's nose a couple degrees north-northeast. He didn't want to accidentally overshoot into the house, but he wanted to do maximum damage to the troops on the balcony. "Firing forward guns," he warned, pressing the fire trigger on the joystick.

Twin Lewis guns spat red tracer fire at the men on the balcony, chewing through their bodies. A single long burst felled the two soldiers behind the planter and the lone shooter by the bronze amphora.

"That's three down..." Doc clenched her fist tightly.

Jack hit his *TALK* button. "Last one, at the end of the balcony, behind that chair."

"Got it," came the reply, followed by the telltale *crack* of a .30-06 Springfield rifle—Charlie's weapon of choice for distance.

Jack watched the target fall in a heap behind the chaise. "Good shootin', Charlie," he said into the headset.

Suddenly, Doc pointed at the mansion's flat roof. "Uh oh," she said.

"Not him again," Jack scowled.

Cipher craned her neck forward to see what they were talking about. "What is it?"

The rooftop shooter from the alley, or someone who looked just like him, was setting up a large rifle on a bipod. He stretched out prone on the sunbaked concrete and took aim.

Jack adjusted for a gust of wind and held down his *TALK* button. "That anti-tank gun from the alley. And he looks loaded for bear. What do you think, Deadeye?"

There was another rifle report, and the gunner's head erupted in a splatter of blood and brains.

Deadeye crackled over the radio. "I think you don't have to worry about him."

Jack and Doc shared a smile, then Jack was back on the radio. "Okay, let's make one more sweep around the property, pick off any more troops sneaking around." He switched off his comms and addressed the women on the bridge. "Cipher, ready the anchor lines and Doc, get set with the ladder."

The turbofans whined as the *Daedalus* ascended and made a couple passes over the property, but no other Silver Star troops were visible.

For the moment, all was quiet.

❧

Within five minutes, the airship was tethered in two places to the wrought iron railing of Marina Stavros' balcony, the crew—minus Rivets—having disembarked and now helping secure and organize the scene. The steel tether cable flexed and contracted with each mild rise and fall of the afternoon breeze. It would have been idyllic if not for the dead bodies, and the bullet in Jack's shoulder.

The Armenian chauffeur helped Deadeye carry one of the Silver Star commandos to where the others had been lined up on the balcony floor, while the butler swept glass and plaster debris into a series of small piles. Marina, unhurt but still a bit shell-shocked from the ordeal, paced the balcony between the bodies and the makeshift surgical theater Doc had improvised. Jack sat backwards on a deck chair, leaning over its back support while

Doc probed the wounded shoulder. The round had penetrated the fleshy muscle of the shoulder blade, and was lodged in the bone itself. Extraction was a pretty straightforward prospect, but a bit awkward with a conscious patient, even numbed as he was.

Marina caught herself mid-pace and finally spoke. "Thank you, my friends."

Jack winced as Doc's steel probe made contact with the bullet. "We couldn't leave you to the Silver Star, Ms. Stavros—ow!"

Doc frowned. "Hold still, or I'll never get this out."

Marina stepped toward the line of corpses as Armen and Deadeye laid out the fifth assailant, the shooter from the roof, before they both wandered back inside. There was a strange odor of sulfur and ozone, and the bodies began to bubble and sizzle, wisps of acrid black smoke wafting skyward.

"So these are the feared agents of the Silver Star."

"Elite troops of some kind," Jack added, wincing again.

"They *were* elite troops of some kind," corrected Doc, pointing them out to Marina. "See how their bodies dissolve when they die?"

Marina Stavros watched their flesh melt as if eaten by acid, withering away to nothing but bone fragments and ash. "I see. Only their uniforms remain."

"We see this happen all the time," Jack explained, feeling a stabbing twinge as Doc grabbed for the bullet with her forceps. "Ow! Jeez, Doc!"

"Quiet, you," she replied tersely.

Marina turned away from the bodies to face the couple. "But why do they disappear?"

"It's so none of their number can ever be taken alive," said Doc. "And their life force joins with Crowley, who grows ever more powerful on the essence of his fallen servants."

The very notion made Marina shudder in disgust and horror.

Deadeye returned to the balcony with arms laden. Jack took immediate notice, and thought an inventory would help distract him from conscious field surgery.

"What'd you find?"

Deadeye dropped his armload of weapons on the floor and nudged each thing with a booted foot. "Four Mauser C96 pistols, two functional MP-18 trench sweepers and that anti-tank T-Gewehr."

Cipher wandered out from the great room and nodded at the powdery remains of the Silver Star troops. She had shed her uniform jacket in favor of the much cooler white tank top underneath. "We can also add two intact Silver Star uniforms," she said, "due to Lieutenant Dalton's superior marksmanship."

Charlie looked at her and blushed, which Cipher took as a small victory.

"Unfortunately, your use of the Lewis guns shredded the others, Captain."

Jack disregarded the jab. "Thanks, Cipher."

"Those may come in handy later," said Doc, indicating the uniforms.

Jack nodded. "Agreed. Go ahead and load up the uniforms, the MP-18s and the anti-tank rifle."

Marina marveled at how calm and collected this crew seemed to be, despite the harrowing afternoon they'd all had. She was impressed. If anyone could hope to stand up to the creeping menace the Silver Star represented, it would be the crew of the airship *Daedalus*. "And when you are done," she smiled, "I insist that you must partake of my promised food and hot baths."

As Doc produced the bullet from Jack's shoulder, her hands slick with his blood and the sweat from this tropical locale, she imagined sliding into a warm stone tub. "With pleasure."

☙

By the time the local constabulary arrived, most of the evidence of the cliffside firefight had been removed. The police sergeant was an old veteran and had questions when he saw the condition of Marina Stavros' great room, but was easily placated with some wine and a stack of cash. There would be no official report. The noise had been "construction" on the foyer, balcony and great room, and a 250-foot airship was certainly *not* tethered outside. The sergeant wasn't actually stretching the law; technically, there were no bodies. Without bodies, there was no crime.

Baths were drawn, clothes laundered and stomachs filled. The *Daedalus* departed just as the sun was setting over the Aegean Sea.

Marina Stavros stood with Fotios the butler and Armen the chauffeur, watching from the balcony as the crew waved from the bridge and sailed away into the evening sky.

Jack kept a low altitude over the Greek islands as Doc plotted a southeast course, ascending to a good cruising altitude as they passed over the isle of Crete. The wind across the Mediterranean was still and silent that night, with nary a headwind nor tailwind to be had.

With course laid in and duty shifts assigned, the *Daedalus* made for the African continent.

- CHAPTER 14 -

Cairo came alive in a prism of color as the sun rose over the Arabian desert. The capital of Egypt and largest metropolis in the Arab world, the ancient city of Cairo was home to a million people, a population dominated by foreign influences—most notably the British, who had ruled the region for generations and used the city as a central garrison during the Great War. Even though the nation of Egypt was technically self-governing these past five years, with nationalist Prime Minister Saad Zaghlul at the helm, its continued status as a British "protectorate" was cause for much conflict—not only in the chambers of its Parliament, but in its boardrooms and back alleys.

As much as Cairo was a powder keg, it was a well-guarded powder keg.

Given the history of western influence in this venerable place, it was no surprise that Cairo was home to an active AEGIS outpost. The sheer number of ancient artifacts of potential mystical power in the region, discovered or otherwise, were beyond counting. Libraries filled with ancient texts and museums displaying the antiquities of human civilization were contained in a city also renowned for its food, entertainment, and hospitality.

Everything a cultured traveler could want was available in Cairo, for the right price. Attractions ran the gamut from the excitement of the horse races to the beauty of the opera house, to thrilling tours of the Great Pyramids or the excavations in the Valley of the Kings, where long-buried treasures had been found, and long-dormant curses triggered.

The rarest of tomes could be found in the dark corners of the Bazaar, while carnal pleasures were made available in Wagh El Birket and other red light districts throughout the sprawling city on the Nile. The black market was so robust as to accommodate pit fights between any combination of human or animal, the trafficking of women and young boys from all over the world, and of course any kind of intoxicant known to mankind. All one need do was ask a local, and if one were lucky, one might actually achieve one's objective without being murdered in the street for one's wallet.

The muezzin call from a dozen minarets rang out over the city as the golden light of morning swept across its face. As the *Daedalus* made its approach over the Nile Delta, it passed over farms, fishing dhows and trading barges, coming in to land at Almaza Air Base on the eastern side of the city. Formerly designated RAF Heliopolis, Almaza was still home to the No. 208 Squadron of British reconnaissance fighters.

Jack whistled approvingly at the row of Bristol F.2 fighters, painted olive drab and sand, with their roundels of red, white and blue on the wings. It was a "Biff" such as these which Jack had "borrowed" from a British pilot called Padger to investigate a hidden thermal valley in the Himalayas. Jack had wrecked Padger's Biff, but AEGIS had secured a replacement in better condition, and now Padger was a field agent with AEGIS in Almora.

It occurred to Jack that he'd developed a habit of "borrowing" other people's vehicles, and wrecking them. Of course, since it was in the service of The Greater Good, it was probably okay, right?

In his extensive travels, Jack had never visited Cairo. To say he was excited was an understatement. In point of fact, none of the crew had been to Cairo before. Cipher had the designation of having come closest, being born a continent away in India. Not even Rivets could be kept in his bunk. As Jack powered down the engines and the British and Egyptian ground personnel helped tie down the sleek airship, the rest of the crew gathered at the port side door. Deadeye flipped the stepladder down, and everyone disembarked into the sweltering African heat.

Jack hopped to the tarmac and immediately beaded up with sweat. He thought his choice of outfit—khakis, boots and a simple shirt with sleeves rolled up—was a good call. This would be a sweltering day. Fortunately the whole crew had a supply of freshly laundered field wear. Doc joined him, her shirt open to the third button and hair tied up in a bandanna. She had a cylindrical chart case slung over her shoulder and her canvas satchel strapped across her body. Deadeye wore his fatigues below and a simple undershirt on top, carbine slung. Cipher helped Rivets down from the gondola steps, wincing in sympathy as his full weight came down on his wounded leg. His overalls were undone to the waist and he'd chosen the same cotton undershirt as Deadeye. His grease-stained cap still sat atop his head, brim shielding his eyes from the tropical sun. Cipher wore a pair of uniform shorts, field boots and a white tank top, having left the crimson beret in her quarters.

Cipher and Rivets joined the other three as the sight of an approaching Crossley troop truck met their eyes.

Jack noticed his mechanic hobbling at his left. "How's the leg?"

"Little gimpy, but I can get around okay," said Rivets, slapping Jack on the back. "How's the shoulder?"

Jack winced as his bandaged shoulder blade took the engineer's hit, radiating a sharp pain across his upper body and down his arm. "Ow! Jeez, Rivets!"

"Sorry," Rivets appeared chastened, and Jack assumed he'd really forgotten.

As a group of uniformed, armed men jumped from the truck and assembled on the tarmac, a well-dressed aristocrat, rosy-cheeked, broad around the middle, possessed of an enormous grin and equally enormous mustache, stepped out of the truck cab. His white cotton suit gleamed in the morning sunlight. The soldiers flanking him were generally young men in khaki shorts and pith helmets.

Doc nodded, addressing her crew mates. "The dapper gent is Sir Harold Marston. Sunday manners, fellas."

Deadeye flashed a half-smile. "Should've worn my special Winchester."

Marston approached, chin high, swagger stick tucked under his armpit. He resembled a formal portrait of King George V, and Jack thought he wouldn't be surprised if Sir Harold and King George were golfing buddies.

Though he wore no uniform, Sir Harold had the bearing of a military man. Heels clicked together as he snapped to attention before the airship crew, the soldiers behind him following suit. "On behalf of the His Majesty King George and the British Empire, I bid you welcome to Egypt!"

Jack held out a hand. "Thank you, sir. I'm —"

"No, don't tell me!" Marston grinned. "I've read about your adventures. 'Captain Stratosphere' Jack McGraw, ace pilot in the Royal Flying Corps during the Big Brawl, eh?"

"I guess that'd be me," Jack flushed.

"And this vision of loveliness is the renowned occult scholar Doctor Dorothy Starr."

Doc found herself in a curtsy before she could catch herself. "Charmed."

Marston turned to Rivets. "Carl Holloway, the mechanical genius behind many of the new AEGIS Aeronautics designs."

"Aww shucks," said Rivets, doffing his cap.

"Charles Dalton, deadliest marksman on the Western Front."

Deadeye nodded. "Sir."

Marston's face brightened an entire shade when he saw Cipher. "And you must be Marissa Singh, the new communications prodigy."

"Sir Harold," Cipher smiled in return.

He turned to regard Jack and Doc. "Bloody awful business in Athens, I hear."

Jack winced slightly, recalling the motorcycle chase through the alleys of Piraeus, taking fire from small arms and anti-tank guns. "It was...a little tense, but nothing we couldn't handle."

Doc stepped closer to Sir Harold. "We were hoping you might have some information for us," she said in hushed tones.

Marston nodded sadly. "The whereabouts of Commander Willis and the *Percival*, I'll wager. I'm afraid not. The ship was due here yesterday. I believe you've been flying Edward's route."

"But a day behind," Jack agreed.

Doc frowned. "Are you sure you haven't heard anything?"

"Nothing official, mind you." Marston winked with an index finger next to his sun-kissed nose. "But why don't we adjourn to my office in the city and you all can clean up, have a drink, and relax awhile."

Rivets eyed the troops standing guard behind Sir Harold. "Hey Cap, shouldn't someone stay with—"

"Safety first, eh, Holloway? Too right!" Marston chortled as he stepped in close to the engineer. "These men are hand-picked and loyal to AEGIS. They'll guard the *Daedalus* while you're away. You have my personal guarantee of her safety while you're in my care."

"Fair enough, Sir Harold," said Jack, gesturing toward the truck. "After you."

"If you don't mind the troop truck," Marston said, almost embarrassed but not quite.

Deadeye smiled broadly. "We're used to it."

Marston saw the crew safely deposited in the canvas-covered bed of the truck, then he hopped in the passenger side of the cab. "Jolly good!"

The truck engine rattled to life, and the driver whisked them away into Cairo.

CR

The office of Sir Harold Marston was a cavernous affair in the Ghamra neighborhood between Shari Hamdi and Avenue de la Reine Nazli. Marston's import-export concern owned the entire building, which doubled as a convenient front for AEGIS operations in the city.

The street-facing half of the ground floor consisted of an exquisitely decorated lobby and reception area, at the center of which percolated a ceramic fountain. The local warehouse took up the back half of the floor, while a variety of commercial and AEGIS-related facilities took up the 2nd, 3rd, and 4th floors. Sir Harold maintained the 5th floor and rooftop garden as his personal office, apartments, and library.

Electric ceiling fans spun slowly on long belts, a token effort to fight the sweltering heat. Marston and the *Daedalus* crew occupied a small corner of the library, content to lounge on white wicker seating or wander about extensive shelves of books and rare manuscripts. Giant potted palms sat in every corner.

Jack perused a row of ancient hand-bound tomes, hands clasped behind his back as he looked, just on the off chance he'd accidentally touch one. "I want to thank you for your hospitality and the use of your library, Sir Harold."

Marston saluted with a fat Omar cigar from his wicker armchair. "An honor and a pleasure, old chap! Glad to be of service in the defense of mankind and all that." His posh received pronunciation was as if the whole of the British Empire itself was speaking through him.

Jack hesitated a moment, then decided to let trust win out. "Sir Harold, how well do you know Colonel Shaw, in the London bureau?"

Doc looked surprised that he would choose this moment to examine his suspicions about Shaw, but she was equally curious to hear Sir Harold's response.

Marston puffed on the Omar and thought for a moment. "Shaw. Stephen Shaw? By jove, you know we served together in the Sudan and later under Allenby in Gaza, during the Great War. Brilliant tactician, good officer. Rather talented wicket-keeper, as I recall. Why do you ask?"

"No reason," said Jack, his suspicions calmed for the moment. "We ran into him in London and I know he'd spent some time out here in the service, and both of you being AEGIS field contacts, thought you might know him."

Jack and Doc exchanged a look, and each decided the matter settled.

Rivets sat semi-reclined, with his wounded leg elevated on a low stool, the rest of his ample frame on a wicker love seat. He sniffed at a small dram of Scotch, rolling it around in the glass before swallowing it down. "Mighty fine whiskey," he said with an added texture to his voice.

"Enjoy it, my good man!" Marston encouraged.

Doc unfurled a large survey map of the Nile region over Sir Harold's massive oak desk. Jack approached behind her, peering over her shoulder as she compared it with a smaller chart from her map case. "This is your most detailed map of the Nile Valley?" she asked.

Marston stood and stretched his arms to the side. "Indeed, Doctor."

Jack eyed Sir Harold as he approached the desk as well. "Back at the airport, you said you didn't have any 'official' information. What did you mean by that?"

Marston bit his lower lip. "Only to say that, while the *Percival*'s destination was officially Cairo, the actual object of study was further down the Nile, in a most inhospitable region just north of Lake Nasser. But that's all I know."

Jack watched as Doc traced the massive river with her index finger, her head snapping up in sudden realization. "Not Naqada."

"The what now?" Jack puzzled.

"It is, isn't it?" Doc's eyes widened. "The Golden City..."

"Hello!" Rivets exclaimed from his seat in the corner.

"Yeah, that got my attention too." Deadeye, who had been leaning against the wall while paging through a book on the French conquest of Africa, was suddenly alert and focused on the desk, the maps, and the conversation.

Marston raised an eyebrow. "Well now, my dear," he said, taking a puff on his cigar. "You may be onto something."

Cipher came out of a row of books and joined the trio at the table, looking over the larger of the maps. "What did you say about a 'golden city'?"

Sir Harold took a giant puff from the Omar, exhaling a series of perfect smoke rings. "Around 3500 B.C., there was a rather thriving city on the West Bank of the Nile, rich in trade from the gold mines of the Eastern Desert." He turned away, scratching his head with the hand holding the cigar. "Devoted to the Cult of Set, if I recall correctly."

"Naqada, huh?" Jack pondered. "Nah-*kah*-duh."

Cipher put a hand on her hip. "If I'm not mistaken, the name derives from the ancient Egyptian *nebu*, meaning gold."

Sir Harold nodded at her. "You are indeed correct, my dear. The Golden City was well-defended by a citadel on a nearby ridge, lousy with temples to Set and teeming with worshipers. Once upon a time, that city was rich as Croesus!"

Jack frowned. "I don't understand. What's there for Duke?"

"Earthquake leveled the place in the first century," Sir Harold explained. "What was left standing was buried by the desert sand over a millennium." He paced the floor next to the desk, trailing thick cigar smoke as he walked. "Despite ample time for grave robbers to clean out the place, rumors persist of treasures remaining in the temples, still hidden due to the hazardous conditions."

Doc wracked her brain, remembering articles and stories she may have read about the place. "Isn't there a village on the site?"

"There have been several, in fact," said Sir Harold. "But between the sandstorms, pestilence, and tribes of bandits in the area, they never last long. The most recent population picked up stakes shortly after the British took over in '82, and the new parliament here hasn't had much time yet to clean up the criminal element along the Nile Valley."

Jack wasn't satisfied with this new potential discovery. "The question remains why Duke hasn't checked in, and why he bypassed Cairo altogether. As I said before, he'd never allow his ship to be boarded."

"Consciously," Doc added.

"What?"

"We know he'd never *consciously* allow it," she explained, "but what if Duke and the crew were under some sort of magical control?"

Deadeye placed his book carefully on an end table and looked seriously at the group. "If Blutig's behind this, we've seen what she can do."

"There's no reason to believe she's behind this," Jack countered.

"There's no reason to believe she's *not*," said Doc. "You know how obsessed she is with taking revenge on you—on all of us."

"Even after we blew up her ship in the Amazon, she rebuilt it and came after us in the Himalayas," recalled Deadeye.

Rivets gulped down another belt of Scotch. "Remember that time she made a whole zeppelin disappear?"

"Yeah, I was shooting at it at the time," said Jack. "So you think Duke and the crew were under Maria's control and just didn't radio in? And if so, what's her game?"

Doc threw a knowing glance Marston's way. "Sir Harold, you mentioned a network of temples to Set?"

"Indeed."

"God of storms, the desert, chaos, and war," she went on.

Jack threw a punch into his open palm. "Right in the Silver Star's wheelhouse."

"And if they have Duke's crew in a temple complex," Doc worried, "who knows what dark magic Maria could be planning?"

"Not to mention stealing our powerplant technology," added Jack.

At that moment, the candlestick telephone on the oak desk rang with two quick alarms. Marston grabbed the stick and plucked the ear piece from its cradle. "Yes?" There was a short pause, and Marston's eyes grew wide. "Affirmative. Well done, chaps." He hung up and replaced the phone on the desk, all eyes riveted on him. "As it happens, the boys in the radio room downstairs picked up Silver Star radio chatter to the southwest of our position, possibly originating in the Eastern Desert."

Cipher leaned forward, pointing at the map. "Then we should be looking for the *Percival* at Naqada."

Jack pressed in next to Doc and flattened the large map on the desktop. "Let me see that map, Doc." He picked up a metal compass, setting it to the proper scale for fifty miles, and stuck one point onto Cairo, walking it down to where Naqada should be. "Less than 300 miles as the crow flies. If we plot our course over the Eastern Desert and push at full speed, we can be there in three hours."

Rivets raised his tiny whiskey glass and cheered. "Amen to that!"

"Let's go get Duke," added Deadeye.

Cipher looked earnestly across the desk at Jack. "I'm ready, Captain."

Jack looked into Doc's green eyes, searching for an answer he already knew.

"You know I'm with you," she said. "Let's go find him."

- CHAPTER 15 -

Within minutes, they were back in the truck, heading up Avenue de la Reine Nazli, dodging the electric tram that ran from the airport into downtown. Doc sat in the cab next to the driver, a young Egyptian soldier by the name of Asim with close-cropped raven hair. Jack sat in the passenger seat, while the rest piled into the covered bed. Jack remembered the look of childlike glee that had erupted on Sir Harold's face when he realized they were about to head out to find the *Percival*. He'd wished the crew "Godspeed," and promised to mobilize all the extra manpower he could muster. But rather than wait for the extra backup, Jack thought it prudent to strike while the iron was hot, with every lost minute a potentially fatal delay for Duke and his crew. As the truck crossed the tram line onto Shari Ghamra, Jack happened to glance in the side mirror.

A snow-white Rolls-Royce Silver Ghost touring car pulled into traffic behind them. The top was down, and four men in what Jack assumed was ceremonial dress sped closer. They were clothed identically, in white cotton *thobe* tunics, with crimson *djellaba* coats and *gallabiya* headscarves, wrapped turban-like around their heads.

"Don't look now," Jack warned the driver of the Crossley. "We've got some new fans."

Asim looked in his side mirror and scowled. "Bloody hell…?"

"They want an autograph?" Doc craned her neck to see across Jack to the passenger side-view mirror.

"I'm gonna find out," said Jack, pulling a single Colt from its holster and opening the passenger door. He stepped onto the running board and slammed the door, hanging onto the truck bed's cover-frame with his left hand. "Heads up," he warned his crew mates through the canvas cover.

Deadeye heard him, and was just about to pull open the tent-like door flap at the rear of the truck bed when the three men in the Rolls who weren't driving suddenly opened up with

MP-18s. Deadeye dove for the bed floor, taking Cipher with him. Rivets fell from the side bench he was sitting on and covered his head as gunfire raked the back of the truck, perforating the canvas cover and splintering holes in the rear panels.

"No kiddin'!" Rivets cried. "Heads up, he says."

Another spray of bullets took away the passenger side mirror, removing Doc's view of the action. Jack snaked his way along the wooden sidewall of the truck bed, keeping his Colt trained on the driver in the Rolls.

"Better tell everyone to hang on," Asim told Doc, who stuck her head out the open passenger window and yelled, "Hang on!"

It was almost a moment too late. The Crossley's brakes squealed under stress and the Rolls plowed into the rear of the truck bed, knocking the Egyptian in the front seat forward, over the windscreen. He landed spread-eagle on the bonnet, scrambled to a kneeling position, and raised his submachine gun to hose down the truck with hot lead.

Suddenly one of the canvas flaps flipped up and the barrel of a Winchester carbine thrust out. It barked once, and the robed gunman slumped, covering the entire hood and windscreen of the Rolls. Deadeye ratcheted the cocking lever forward and braced to fire a second time, but at that moment, the truck driver stepped on the gas, and the Crossley roared forward. Jack was just getting to the back of the sidewall, and the lurch forward knocked him off balance. He fell, coming to an abrupt landing on top of the gunman on the bonnet of the Rolls.

Not wanting to lose the truck, the robed driver stepped on the gas, looking over the two bodies on the hood of his car to steer. For a moment, Jack lay still, face down and staring at the two gunmen in the back seat. They stared back.

Finally, one of them pulled back the bolt on his submachine gun, and Jack knew he was not likely to make it out of this chase alive if he did nothing. Moving from his prone position into a crouch, he leaped, clearing the windscreen and landing on the dark red leather bench seat in front.

The gunman on his left raised his MP-18 and fired a long burst at Jack's head. Jack ducked away and spun between the two, coming to a landing on the slightly angled boot of the Rolls. He was now behind them, looking forward. The driver looked up, their eyes meeting in the rear view mirror. Jack stepped into the lap of the man who had fired at his head—now on his right—pinning the man's gun under his weight. His right elbow rocketed down and met the bridge of the gunman's nose. The man fell back with a wince, spewing blood from his nostrils. In the same motion, Jack punched forward with his gun hand, coming around to level his Colt in the second gunman's face. The second gunman, who had just pulled back the bolt on his submachine gun, lowered the weapon, pointing it at Jack's center of mass. Both men froze in place.

Time slowed to a crawl as the Rolls sped through the Cairo thoroughfare. Jack was standing in the back seat as the car whipped through traffic, trying to close distance with the truck. One foot was in the lap on the first gunman, keeping his MP-18 out of commission. The other foot braced him precariously between the first man and the man who now held the ready gun at his chest.

Jack put his hands up in surrender, noting in his periphery the Winchester barrel once again protruding from the canvas flaps of the Crossley. Another shot rang out, and the gunman's MP-18 was torn from his hands. It spun away into the busy street. The Rolls driver stepped on the brakes and threw Jack off balance long enough for the first gunman to rip his MP-18 from under Jack's boot. As he turned the weapon toward the small of Jack's back, a third shot exploded from the Winchester, and the gunman flipped back over the boot of the Rolls, gun flung into the street. The

Rolls driver stomped on the gas again. This time the lurch gave Jack extra momentum as he spun to face front—his left hand balled into a fist which caught the second gunman in a powerful cross. The robed man slumped against the back seat door, dazed.

Jack now sat facing forward, watching the driver watch *him* through the mirror. He suddenly felt a tightness close around his throat, tension pulling back on his windpipe. He couldn't breathe, but as his eyes rolled back in his head, he knew it was the wounded gunman on the boot. By instinct, his right hand flew back directly over his head and he fired the Colt upside down at point-blank range. The garrote slipped from his neck and the man flopped from the back of the car like a dead salmon.

Just then, the second gunman shook off his stupor and pulled a *jambiya* dagger from its silver sheath at his belt. Jack saw the flash of sunlight off the blade and his left hand snapped out to grab the man's knife arm. He pulled hard, wrenching the man forward, and shoved the Colt under his extended torso. Three gunshots emptied into the man's gut. As he thrust the dead weight off him, he noticed a tattoo on the inside of the man's forearm. He'd eventually want to recreate it for Doc and see what she had to say, but first, he had to get out of this speeding Rolls and back onto the truck.

His right shoulder erupted in blood and for a moment he didn't feel any pain. He just stared at the smoking barrel of the Mauser pistol the driver held across his chest, pointing into the back seat. But then another shot rang out, and the driver's hand released the pistol, a bloody hole placed dead center. He screamed in anguish, returning his attention to the road.

Jack looked up and saw Cipher with her own smoking revolver, kneeling in the truck bed. She aimed and fired again—this shot hit the driver in the forehead. He slumped forward over the wheel, and Jack could feel the accelerator press under the dead man's weight.

At the same time the truck began to slow again, and Jack knew a crash was imminent.

Disregarding the throbs of pain and blood gushing from his previously good shoulder, he stood on the back seat, pushing off from the seat back of the front bench seat, with one foot, he managed to clear the windscreen. One leap with his other foot from the hood of the Rolls and he was airborne, as the speeding car made contact with the bed of the Crossley, turned hard to the right and careened into oncoming traffic. Jack flew through the canvas door of the truck and rolled onto the wood floor, flat on his back.

Rivets, Cipher and Deadeye peered over him as he lay still, breathing heavily. Blood seeped from his new wounds as well as his bandaged shoulder. He blinked his eyes open and started to say something.

"I wouldn't," Deadeye said quietly. "Let us get you back to the ship and checked out."

"Been a day, hasn't it, Cap?" Rivets chuckled.

"Yeah," Jack replied. "It certainly has been a day."

ʘ

The truck pulled into Almaza and came to a stop on the tarmac a few yards from the *Daedalus*. Asim helped Deadeye, Doc, and Cipher carry Jack aboard the airship and into the main saloon. Doc began to examine him while Rivets limped back to the engine room, and Cipher went forward to the bridge. Flushed and sweating, Asim bid the crew farewell, telling them he hoped they'd meet again. Deadeye stayed at Doc's side to assist if needed.

The bullet had gone clear through Jack's shoulder, so there was nothing to dig out, thank heavens. In minutes, he was cleaned up with two bandaged shoulders—he even managed to get a in a dig about Doc wanting to get his shirt off. She waited until Deadeye had gone topside to the turret before she planted a big kiss on him.

"Don't go leaping on cars in traffic," she scolded. "It's a miracle you weren't killed."

"Crazy and dangerous," he replied. "It's what we do."

Doc helped Jack into a clean khaki shirt, and they went forward to the bridge to power up the ship and prepare for takeoff.

"Ground crew is ready to cast off," Cipher relayed.

At the nav station, Jack found the red wax pencil Doc used for plotting courses. "Borrow your notebook?" he asked.

Doc dug into her satchel and pulled out an 8" x 5" leather-covered journal with an elastic band around it. Removing the band, she opened the book to a blank page, and watched as Jack drew a hieroglyph: a left-facing person, seated, with some kind of animal head.

"Is that a jackal?" she asked.

Jack shook his head no. "The nose was long and curved, almost like an anteater."

Doc nodded. "Ah, right. That's Set."

Cipher looked at the drawing and sighed. "So we have cultists of Set after us as well?"

"Well, we *are* heading to Naqada," Doc shrugged. "They may have been trying to send us a message."

Jack wasn't satisfied with that explanation. "Nobody knows that's where we're going, except the five of us and Sir Harold." He stepped down to the pilot's chair and sat, fishing a stick of gum out of his pants pocket. "No, it's far more likely these goons were working with the Silver Star. If they were sent to keep us away from Naqada, then it's a sure sign that's exactly where they are." He hit the *TALK* switch on the comms and his voice echoed throughout the ship. "Captain to crew—secure the ship and prepare for takeoff. We're heading to Naqada, which means almost certain hostile action with forces of the Silver Star. I need everyone at their best." He paused, adding, "Duke needs us. Captain out."

The thrust engines spun to life, ground tethers cast off, and the *Daedalus* rose into the noonday Egyptian sky.

ଔ

The blindfold came off, and Duke squinted as the white-hot desert sun met his eyes. He was standing just outside the shadow of the *Percival*. The airship was anchored to a crevasse in the rocky canyon surrounding them, only scant meters from a massive—no, *two* massive airships stretching hundreds of feet into the distance. He recognized the four-pointed star insignia on them, and on the caps and collars of the soldiers corralling him.

It was just about high noon, he estimated, and it appeared he and his crew were being moved from the *Percival* to one of two transport trucks parked nearby. His crew members marched ahead of him, each bound in front with strong cord. Duke could see his navigator, Lucille Pimm, with blond hair pulled back above her shoulders. After her went Morgan Evans, his radio officer, a dark-haired Welshman, then chief engineer Henry Lee, a bespectacled black mechanic recruited from the Canadian Air Force. Brothers Gerald and Jonathan Wincott followed, both gunners and pathfinders with the Royal Army before signing with AEGIS. Gerald was suave and dark-haired like Duke, with Jonathan a bit older, redder and rounder, overly-generous mutton chops swathing his face.

Duke reached up with his bound hands and rubbed at his jaw, bristly with days of beard. He felt the sweat trickle down from his forehead, and cursed the lack of his officer's cap.

It certainly felt like Egypt, given the oppressive sun and arid terrain. He wished he could remember the past few days, but everything after the electrical storm over the Italian Alps was a blank. The only thing he knew for sure was that this was a big operation, possibly bigger than the Amazon project had been for the Silver Star. As they crossed the dusty ridge floor toward the open truck, Duke renewed his hopes for a rescue from his friends —who had no idea where he was.

- CHAPTER 16 -

Under a less pressing timetable, Jack would have preferred to take a leisurely flight following the twists and turns of the mighty Nile to their destination. In this case, however, time was absolutely of the essence, so a straight course was set south-southeast across the foreboding strip of desert between the Nile and the Gulf of Suez.

With one generator down, Jack could hope to push the ship to a top speed of 100 miles per hour, but anything more, like the radio detector, would put too much drain on the electrical system. Or at least that's what he thought.

At the end of the first hour, Rivets announced over the comms that the passive solar receptors in the airship's vulcanized dura-lumin skin were topping off the battery array quite nicely, soaking up the bright sunlight of northern Africa. Jack replied that he could kiss Rivets. The mechanic, flattered, politely declined.

By the end of the second hour, Cipher had picked up some unusual readings to the southwest. There was lots of radio chatter on the Silver Star's chosen frequency, and some structures, or vehicles, partially hidden in a valley behind a small rocky ridge in the Eastern Desert.

Jack mused to himself. In the war, he'd gained the nickname Captain Stratosphere from the dogfighting tactic of starting at the upper limit of his plane's service ceiling, keeping the sun behind him. It was a great vantage from which to see enemy aircraft while staying clear of ground fire. Enemies would often be caught off-guard by the ace pilot and his squadron as they screamed down from the heavens. He'd flown the *Daedalus* higher than any other aircraft in his career, and wished he could do so again, but this situation called for different tactics.

No, they would have to come in low, to keep as hidden as one could possibly be if one were a 250-foot electric airship. If the Silver Star had captured the *Percival*, they would probably be using its radio detector, so the lower the *Daedalus* could fly, the better.

They almost skimmed the Nile surface as the airship came in low from the northeast. Jack throttled down and banked into a right turn as they hooked around the southern tip of a small island and nosed past a line of palms.

Centuries of sandstorms and erosion had covered whatever had once stood along this riverbank. Massive dunes sloped from a ridge line about three miles west, trailing all the way to the reedy edge of the Nile. Even so, Jack thought he could see the remnants of ancient columns thrust up from the sand like the arms of a drowning man.

"Let's see if we can find an anchorage up near that ridge," he said.

After ten minutes of fighting the eastbound winds and ever-present hiss of sand blasting the envelope of the *Daedalus*, Jack turned the ship back to the west bank of the Nile, where they could drop behind the palms and be assured of secure anchorage and a radio detection screen. "We'll have to go on foot," he admitted as the engines shut down and the crew unharnessed.

Doc unfurled a Royal Survey map of the area. It was from the 1880s, but it had most of the relevant topographical features accounted for. From their current position, it was a three-mile hike across rolling sand dunes to the first ridge. That was the most likely location of the entrance to the temple complex.

Beyond the first ridge was an open plain a mile across, which shattered into a million canyons and rocky outcrops, perfect for hiding large airships and sundry military hardware. This was where Cipher had picked up the large objects. Whatever Maria Blutig was doing here—if it was indeed her—was a bigger operation than they'd ever encountered.

The crew gathered by the rear hatch in the main gantry. Rivets powered the ladder down while Deadeye, Jack, and Doc readied their gear, dressing in the pilfered Silver Star uniforms.

"Rivets, you stay on the stick. Keep her low and away from the ridge, and if trouble comes looking, get out of here."

"Aye, Cap."

Jack popped the magazines out of each Colt to check ammo, slapping each back in with a click. "Cipher, you stay on comms. I'll key my transceiver handset three times if we need support."

"Affirmative," she replied.

Doc looked into her satchel and reassured herself that the bronze vambrace from Marina Stavros remained inside. The lodestone dangled from her neck, her Colt police special holstered at her hip. "Deadeye," she said. "Let's bring some of that new hardware."

Deadeye adjusted the flat commando cap on his head. "It's all in the duffel."

"Then let's get going," said Jack, as he disappeared through the hatch.

Doc followed, then Deadeye, shouldering the heavy duffel with a grunt.

The *Daedalus* hovered steadily near the water's edge, while the shore party ducked through the line of palm trees and began their three-mile trudge across the sand dunes to the rock ridge above.

ॐ

Duke opened his eyes for a moment, catching the warmth of torchlight off the ornately-painted murals and hieroglyphs. The air was thick and foul in here. He knew they were somewhere deep underground, and that this chamber was central to the temple network of Set.

To his left, Pimm and Lee knelt, still bound and under guard by several Silver Star commandos with submachine guns. To his right, Gerald Wincott knelt with downcast eyes. The chamber they were in was perhaps sixty feet in diameter, with twenty-foot ceilings and a second-floor gallery which covered three of the four walls. Painted columns ran floor to ceiling, and nearest the prisoners at the head of the room lay a raised dais, with an obelisk at each end, and a painted altar in the center.

Duke suddenly realized that chained to each of the obelisks was one of his crew, Morgan Evans and Jonathan Wincott, respectively.

And striding to the altar, parting the throng of cultists who had gathered to participate, was a tall woman with short-bobbed raven hair, who Duke knew quite well. She wore black mystic's robes trimmed in crimson, and carried a familiar cobra-headed staff.

"Maria Blutig," Duke muttered as scattered memories of the past three days washed over him.

She heard the utterance and turned to look at Duke, a psychotic smile piercing the haze and gloom of the subterranean temple. "You remember me!" she gasped, balling her unencumbered hand into a tight fist that shook with excitement. "Good."

She turned to Morgan Evans, who was barely conscious, pumped full of opiates and having undergone two solid days of interrogation and torture. "*Herr* Evans," she addressed, "pledge your loyalty to the Astrum Argentum and our most enlightened master, Aleister Crowley."

Evans turned, his head wobbling weakly on his neck. The cold stone of the obelisk almost felt good on his back. He was parched, but he managed to work up enough spit to launch into Maria's face.

"Very well," said Maria matter-of-factly, wiping the foam from her cheek with the sleeve of her vestments. In a single motion, she drew a ceremonial dagger from its scabbard at her belt and slashed the blade across Evans' throat. It took a moment, then the bloody hole dropped open, blood gushing out onto the temple floor. It ran into an intricate maze of troughs and carvings in the floor, spreading ahead of his feet like a tsunami wave, disappearing into various holes before Evans, pale and empty, slumped dead against the chains holding him to the obelisk.

"No!" Duke caught himself protesting just before the rumbling started. It worked its way from deep underground, up into the temple complex itself, a tremor that burst forth from the earth, followed by the linen-wrapped, desiccated arm of someone long dead. A second arm appeared, then a head, and a body close behind.

Duke realized at that moment that Maria had sacrificed Evans in order to resurrect a mummy. But the tremor didn't stop. A second mummy erupted from the sand, and a third.

Maria smiled as the animated corpses staggered to standing positions flanking the cultists in front. She turned to Jonathan Wincott on the other obelisk as her soldiers unchained Evans and dragged his body away. Another two soldiers came for Gerald Wincott, hauling him to the now vacant, blood-stained obelisk. Maria tutted as she drew nearer to Jonathan's face. "You can save your life, Mr. Wincott, and that of your brother, if you will but pledge your soul to the Astrum Argentum and our master."

She then realized the extra leverage she had in the new victim being chained to the other obelisk. She looked at Gerald, then back at Jonathan. "Should I ask your younger brother the same question?" Drawing the bloody blade of the dagger across her lips, Maria strode over to Gerald. The young man was sobbing, delirious. He kept looking down at the red-stained temple floor beneath him and shivering.

"Gerald," Maria said softly, trying to find his gaze. "Will you pledge your soul to the Astrum Argentum and to Master Magus Aleister Crowley, the Great Beast of Mankind?"

Jonathan struggled at his chains. "Give her nothing, little brother!"

Gerald raised his head long enough to stammer, "N-no…"

Without a word, Maria's blade slashed, and Gerald Wincott bled out onto the floor.

The elder Wincott gave an animal cry and yanked against the chains binding him to the stone obelisk. He didn't even notice another tremor within the earth, or the appearance of another three linen-wrapped corpses.

Duke couldn't believe what he was seeing. He knew that the Silver Star often used human sacrifice in their rituals, and that they'd saved dozens of natives from the knife when they disrupted Crowley's summoning in the Amazon. But this seemed like small potatoes.

"Is this all we are to be?" Duke begged. "Blood sacrifices to summon the dead to your service?"

Maria whirled to face Duke. "Oh, Commander Willis," she chuckled maniacally. "I am just warming up. The rest of you are to be the sacrifice to summon Ammit, the Soul-Eater."

Instantly sorry he asked, Duke's head slumped as the temple suddenly filled with ominous, unearthly chanting. Gerald's body was freed from the pillar and piled next to Evans in the corner.

The soldiers came and wrestled Lee to his feet for a short walk to the well-used obelisk, and Maria Blutig returned her attention to

Jonathan Wincott, running the dagger's blade softly down the side of his head.

"Well?" she whispered enticingly.

"Get stuffed," Jonathan Wincott spat, as his throat opened in a fountain of crimson.

- CHAPTER 17 -

They were perhaps two hundred yards short of the ridge when Jack felt a strange vibration that emanated from the sand dunes and up into his feet. "Hold up," he said, cocking his head to the wind. "Do you hear that?"

The low hum of twenty voices rumbling in unison seeped from the ground as water from a spring. It made the hairs on the backs of their necks stand up, and perhaps more frightening, it produced an almost hypnotic, soporific effect.

"Sounds like chanting," offered Deadeye.

Doc held her palms down toward the dunes and noticed the lodestone was glowing a faint but distinct blue. "It's coming from down there. Beneath us."

The three of them plodded toward the harder soil of the temple ruins, coming across a partially demolished labyrinth of earthen walls and foundations. Everywhere they looked, potential entry points had been caved in and covered in debris and sand.

Jack pointed out a large pile of stones and toppled columns, and an arch which looked like it had been pried off the front of a huge structure and snapped in half. "That main temple entrance is buried. They must have found another entry."

Deadeye flagged them from his vantage at a low wall to the north. He was peering at something through his field glasses. "Over here," he said. Doc and Jack joined him at the wall, and he pointed to the ridge wall about a hundred yards distant. "Leeward side of the ridge. Take a peek at that." He handed his binoculars to Jack, and Doc pulled her own pair from her satchel.

Two Silver Star commandos armed with MP-18s stood guard by a nondescript opening in the rock face. On the flat next to the ridge, two German-built troop trucks stood empty.

"Well lookie there," Jack muttered. "Think that might be our way in?"

Doc nodded. "Absolutely. I'm just a bit nervous about the number of troops inside the complex."

"That makes all three of us," said Jack. He turned to Charlie and patted his shoulder. "Deadeye, find some high ground and keep the trucks covered with the T-Gewehr if we need a distraction. Doc and I will neutralize the guards, then you follow us inside and watch our six."

Deadeye nodded. "You got it." And then he was off, scrambling around boulders and collapsed columns, hurdling over wall fragments like a dressage horse.

"Come on, Doc," Jack waved, standing up straight and walking toward the guards as if he was absolutely supposed to be there. Doc followed, hoping the commandos would recognize two of their own, due to the stolen uniforms.

Deadeye took up a position due east of the entrance, at a distance of 150 yards. He found a partial wall made of ancient bricks that was almost comfortable to lie across, as he pulled the anti-tank rifle from the big duffel bag and braced it on the debris in front of him. Peering through the scope, he could see the trucks plainly, each parked nose-out to the east. He would have no problem landing a shot in the engine block.

As Jack and Doc approached, Jack waved at the guards as if returning from a patrol. He hoped it would be that easy.

But of course it wasn't.

Both commandos unslung their submachine guns and raised them to aim at the incoming "soldiers".

"*Halt!*" ordered the first one.

"Oh, hello, boys!" Doc smiled as she walked up between them, hand on the grip of the Mauser C96 pistol that was holstered but un-secured at her hip.

"*Kommen sie hier!*" the second one barked in German, waving the barrel of his MP-18 to gesture Jack forward.

Jack stepped toward the first guard without telegraphing the brutal right cross he planted on the commando's chin. "'Scuse me, Fritz!" There was a *pop* as the commando's jaw dislocated and the man fell unconscious, while Jack shook out his bruised hand.

"Can't forget his friend," Doc said as she took advantage of the second guard's shift in attention. Pulling the Mauser from its holster, she swung the butt of the pistol upward from below his nose. A brief squirt of blood erupted from the man's face as he fell backward to the ground.

"Nice pistol whip, Doc."

"Why thank you, Captain."

Jack turned to signal an OK to Deadeye, but Charlie was more concerned with the pair of commandos who had just come from the second truck to investigate the commotion.

"Hey! What's going on?" demanded the first soldier, leveling his own MP-18 at Jack and Doc.

"Come over here!" ordered the second one, right hand dropping toward a belt holster.

Jack raised his hands in surrender. "It's okay. It's not what you think—"

The first truck exploded into a fireball of metal, wood, and canvas, shredding apart the first soldier and knocking the second backward to the dirt.

Jack and Doc ducked away instinctively, looking back at the burning truck in surprise. The second soldier staggered to a wide stance, reaching again for his sidearm. The second truck erupted in fire and smoke much like the first, perforating the soldier with shards of glass windscreen and metal bits from the truck body.

All four of the Silver Star soldiers began to sizzle and smoke with that familiar acidic, sulfur smell.

Doc blinked and turned toward the source of the exploded trucks: Deadeye approached, gripping his Winchester, enigmatic Mona Lisa smile across his suntanned face.

"Whoa!" she gasped.

As Charlie walked up, Jack clapped him on the shoulder. "Good shootin', Deadeye. Nobody's leaving in those trucks now."

"So much for the element of surprise," Doc shrugged.

Jack tugged one of his Colts from its holster and waved a dismissive hand. "Eh, they're all underground, chanting."

"They probably have other troops up above, keeping watch," Doc retorted.

Jack laughed. "You worry too much."

"If you say so," Doc sighed. "Shall we?"

"After you," Jack bowed with a flourish.

Doc led the way as they entered the carved opening in the ridge wall. Rough hewn stairs immediately banked left and descended deep into the ground. Jack pulled a flashlight from his pack and shone it on the staircase as the three of them followed it down. The low hum of the occult chant reverberated through the chambers and passages, and the lodestone around Doc's neck pulsed blue-white light.

Down the stairway led. Ever downward.

☙

Cipher adjusted the dial of the radio detector, watching the wave ripple outward from the *Daedalus* and wash over the ridges and hills in the local vicinity. Something huge was moving on the plateau above the first ridge.

"Commander, I've got an object the size of the carrier *Osiris* leaving the second ridge!"

Rivets frowned behind his prominent gray mustache, holding the airship low and steady from the pilot's seat. "We won't be engaging that monster," he said. "But keep an eye on its heading and watch for any more movement up on the plateau."

Cipher nodded. "Affirmative." She adjusted the wave, tightening focus on the *Osiris* as it ascended. "*Osiris* is climbing, heading south-southeast."

Rivets gave a heavy sigh, fidgeting at the stick. "Aw, hell," he grumbled.

"Commander?"

Rivets turned to look at Cipher out of the corner of his eye. "Lieutenant," he said, "are you as curious as I am to find out what the *Osiris* left behind on that ridge?"

"I have been able to make out at least one other large craft."

"Yeah, we assume that's the *Luftpanzer II*. But where the hell are they hiding the *Percival*?"

"They may not be hiding it at all," offered Cipher. "The *Percival* may well be anchored in the same canyon—it just might be hidden by the rock formations in the ridge, and over-shadowed by the *Luftpanzer.*"

"Yeah?" Rivets asked, scratching his head under his sweat-stained cap. "Well, I wanna find out for sure."

Cipher blinked, brown eyes wide. "But sir, the Captain ordered us to stay out of trouble."

"I'll keep us out of trouble," said Rivets with far more conviction than he meant. "Let's go have a look-see."

Throttling up and edging back on the stick, Rivets urged the *Daedalus* into the sky. In less than four minutes, the airship had climbed to an altitude of about 200 feet and crossed the three miles of dunes to the first ridge.

Rivets scanned the ground through the bridge window panels, noting the smoldering remains of two troop trucks and a handful of Silver Star soldiers. "Looks like Captain Stratosphere and Company have been here."

Cipher adjusted the dial on the detector once again. "Commander, if you swing us around to the south and west, I may be able to narrow the band and locate the *Percival.*"

"Can do!" came Rivets' enthusiastic reply, and he leaned over on the stick while throt-tling to reverse speed. The giant electric thrusters flipped over in response, pushing the *Daedalus* backward and over the first ridge into the Eastern Desert.

From their altitude, Rivets could make out part of the torpedo shape of the redesigned *Luftpanzer*, now an aerocarrier in and of itself, with a flattened runway along her dorsal edge. She was parked on the canyon floor, 1000 feet long and over 100 wide, black and silver skin gleaming in the desert sun. "Would ya look at that..." Rivets mused, considering the mechanical engineering feat that was an airship like the *Luftpanzer*.

"Sir," Cipher hailed. "I have it!"

"Right there with ya, Cipher." Rivets continued his swing in reverse over the lip of the canyon, and there behind the second ridge was the *Percival*, anchored to the ground not a hundred feet from the *Luftpanzer*. "She doesn't look damaged," Rivets appraised. "Still, I'd love to get a look from the ground."

"Commander, you can't be thinking—"

"You see any troops down there?"

Cipher was beside herself. She was an AEGIS flight officer, steeped in procedure and protocol. And currently her commander was a curmudgeonly mechanic who was used to improvisation on the battlefield.

In Rivets' defense, she didn't see any soldiers wandering about the canyon floor, but that didn't necessarily mean there weren't any skulking around out of their view.

"Here's the plan," offered Rivets as he shrugged out of the pilot's harness. "You take the stick. Get me to thirty, forty feet above the *Percival*, and I can get in through the top hatch. If she's sky-worthy, we can get both these beauties in the air in case our friends need an emergency rescue."

Cipher's mouth went dry. "But I—"

"You're qualified on the LR-3, right?"

"Well, yes, I'm rated as—"

"Great! Take over. I'm going to the front belly hatch."

Cipher noticed he'd already let go of the stick. Quickly she set her headset on the comms panel and jumped down to the pilot's chair, strapping in. "Oh no..."

And with that, Rivets left the bridge, stopping at the forward hatch to unfurl an aluminum chain ladder, identical to the one at the rear.

He opened the round hatch door inward, letting it fall on the gantry floor. Looking down through the opening, he could see the canyon wall and the *Percival* sitting next to it.

Cipher throttled down just short of full-stop, descending over the edge of the canyon as Rivets let the ladder drop. The ship fell gracefully under the power of the thrust engines, which spun to face a downward direction, pushing ever closer toward the ground.

Slinging an MP-18 over his shoulder, Rivets found his initial footing on a metal rung and began his own descent down the dangling ladder. The *Daedalus* came to a stop, hovering just thirty feet above the *Percival*. Rivets continued, hand over hand, foot over foot, down the ladder.

He was twelve feet above the spine of the *Percival* when three Silver Star commandos wandered out from the shadow of the smaller airship and saw Rivets hanging in the air above them.

An angry exchange of bullets and profanity followed.

- CHAPTER 18 -

The tunnel extended down a hundred yards of carved steps before terminating in a T. One end of the corridor went right and disappeared into darkness, while the other went left in a gentle curve and seemed to be lit from the occasional torch sconce. Ancient pictographs from the earliest parts of Egyptian history lined the walls and wrapped the support columns in black, red, and green.

"These hieroglyphs are amazing," Doc noted. "The Cult of Set is among the earliest forms of organized worship in the pre-dynastic period."

"We can sightsee another time, Doc," said Jack impatiently. "Which way?"

Deadeye paused at the bottom of the stairway, listening to sounds outside. "I hear gunfire."

"Sir Harold might have brought reinforcements," Jack shrugged.

Doc pointed to the left passage curving down and away. "This corridor continues downward, I'd assume to the main temple."

"Then that's where we go," Jack said, leading the way. He flicked off the flashlight and put it back in his pack. Both Colts came out as he trudged down the corridor.

Doc remembered the vambrace in her satchel and stopped to put it on. It fit her left forearm like it had been made specifically for her. "Now, what was that invocation?" she mumbled, thinking back to the book on ancient Greek magic she'd found in Sir Harold's library. "*Athiná me prostatéfsei sti máchi.*"

The corridor was suddenly illuminated in a greenish-blue glow as a bubble of light erupted from the armor cuff and surrounded Doc. Jack noticed, and turned to backtrack a few paces to see what was wrong.

"What the—? What did you do?" Jack demanded, as Deadeye looked on from the rear.

Doc smiled, examining the glowing vambrace with wide eyes. "I found it in a book in Sir Harold's library." The lodestone around her neck glowed white with an ethereal hum.

"Too bad you didn't know that back in Piraeus," Jack scoffed. "You know, when I was getting shot."

Doc cracked a wry half-smile. "There you go again," she chuckled. "Always dwelling in the past."

They walked in silence for a minute before coming to another T-junction, only this was more like a C-junction, with the two branches of the corridor curving away in a graceful, hand-carved arc. An archway on the right led through to a terrace beyond.

Jack holstered his pistols and slung his pack around to his front to access what was inside. "Deadeye, head down to the left and see if there's another doorway on that side," he nodded down the corridor while producing a coiled length of rope. "Doc and I will go through this one."

"Right," Charlie nodded, stalking quietly down the hall while ratcheting the lever of the Winchester in preparation.

Jack and Doc moved to either side of the arch. The light from the lodestone cast everything in a blue tint, and Doc seemed transfixed. The last and only time she'd seen it react this strongly was during Crowley's summoning in the Amazon, when she invoked the powerful Cross of Cadiz to vanquish a demon called Choronzon. "Look at this," she whispered. "The lodestone is glowing like crazy."

"I'm looking," said Jack softly. "There's already some strong magic at work here."

She knew he meant the ancient vambrace around her arm, but that wasn't even the tip of the magical iceberg. The stone had been glowing brightly throughout their journey down the staircase. There was far more powerful magic at work down here.

She caught his gaze and held it for a brief moment. "You ready?"

"Not really," said Jack. "But when has that ever stopped us?"

Together they passed under the arch and found themselves in the gallery above the main temple, overlooking a scene of unbelievable horror.

CR

Cipher felt the release of tension as the *Daedalus* suddenly became 200 pounds lighter. Rivets had jumped—or fallen—from the ladder onto the spine of the *Percival*. She spun the airship and nosed down to get the best view she could manage, and saw the tiny form of Rivets running along the sister ship's topside, stopping to fire a short burst at a soldier popping up through her dorsal hatch.

Keeping the *Daedalus* nose-down, she flicked the console switch to enable the fire-linkage from the front turret to the joystick. She swept sidelong in a lateral pass, taking note of several commandos scurrying around the canyon interior. Not wanting to cause unnecessary damage to the *Percival*, Cipher backed off, daring the squad of commandos to follow.

Follow they did, firing their submachine guns at the airship as it backed along the canyon rim. Abruptly, Cipher nosed the ship forward, squeezing the trigger. A volley of red tracer fire lit up the shade of the ridge, ripping through four of the commandos as another two dove aside.

She only had about two seconds to feel proud of herself before the telltale sound of a Fokker C.V fighter's engine erupted to the west. It climbed into the air from the runway atop the *Luftpanzer,* the growl distinctive as it ascended. She heard the roar of its Panther engine, heard it whine as it rolled over on its back, and dove.

Cipher panicked. She couldn't solo a dogfight with a single fighter plane, let alone more than one. She pulled back on the stick and the ship's nose came up just as the C.V-D made it's run. Green flashes of light streaked by as the fighter unleashed its 7.2 millimeter machine guns on the much slower and larger target.

Miraculously, the enemy pilot overshot, and had to put some distance between them before turning for another pass. Cipher took the opportunity to pull back hard on the stick and throttle to full-speed, rising into the sky on an escape heading. As she climbed, she leaned a bit right on the stick, edging away from the canyon. She didn't want to leave Rivets down there alone, but she also knew a crashed airship was no good to the crew. Besides, it was Commander Holloway's idea to leave the ship in a hotbed of enemy activity.

Unable to take any readings from the radio detector at the comms station, Cipher had to fly and shoot by sight and instinct. The *Daedalus* continued to climb into the hot afternoon sky. Cipher hoped she'd been given enough of a head start to outlast her pursuers.

A squadron of fighters appeared on the northern horizon, and Cipher's breath caught in her throat.

CR

Rivets shoved the dead man down the ladder to the gantry below. He quickly scanned the airship's interior before scampering down faster than his frame would indicate the ability to. If he could get to the bridge without getting killed, he could power up the *Percival's* engines and join Cipher in the air.

As his boots hit the aluminum deck, he heard heavy machine gun fire outside, and wondered if Cipher had found the fire-link controls on the pilot's console. He slunk carefully toward the aft section of the airship, staying low as he moved through the main saloon. Noticing the engine room door hatch open, he stepped inside to take stock.

The gauges and battery array looked good, but there was something amiss with the frictionless dynamos, ten of which were normally wired in sequence. Rivets did a quick count, noting a vacant slot at the bottom corner.

The tenth dynamo was missing.

Drat, thought Rivets. *They already removed a generator.* That would make it a useless task to arm the self-destruct mechanism. Instead, he thought the *Percival* might be of more use in the air, where he could at least strafe the Silver Star soldiers on the ground with the forward guns.

He made his way forward to the main salon, peeking through the array of gondola windows to see groups of gray-clad soldiers and black-uniformed officers run to and fro as the general alarm was raised. He'd have to do this very carefully. With the MP-18 held at waist height against any potential opponent, Rivets poked his head onto the bridge.

It was empty.

Moving quickly, the mechanic moved to the pilot's seat and shouldered his gun. He began flipping switches, listening to the hum of turbofans powering on. A distinctly mechanical roar erupted from outside, and Rivets knew the Silver Star were putting planes in the sky.

Damn, he thought. *I need to get this baby up and away, pronto.*

"You will drop your weapon and power the engines down, please," came a businesslike command with an officer-class German accent.

Rivets turned. Standing in the bridge hatchway was Captain Jonas Ecke, a Luger pistol pointing from his right hand. Flanking him were two Silver Star commandos, armed and ready.

A look of recognition came over Ecke's face and he smiled through his magnificent white beard. "I remember you. You were the mechanic aboard the *Daedalus*, who we captured in the Amazon."

"Still am," Rivets replied, un-shouldering his weapon and letting it fall to the deck.

Captain Ecke smiled a little less, and waved the Luger, directing Rivets toward the exit. "Maybe so, but not for much longer," he warned. "You will please come with us now."

Rivets switched off the engine power, put his hands up, and the commandos marched him off the bridge.

⌘

Doc and Jack peered over the short gallery wall into the temple below. They could see through the firelight and hazy interior to the center dais, with the altar at the top and the obelisks to each side. Jack noticed a person chained to each obelisk, and a neatly organized pile of corpses to the right. Doc tried to scan through the murky atmosphere, but could not make out the chained figures.

Jack counted between a dozen and twenty robed cultists. In his experience, they were devout and might have a knife or a magic trick up their black and crimson sleeves, but they were a comparatively low threat level. The commandos, however—two at each of three lower doors, armed to the teeth—were a different story. And that didn't even begin to cover whatever those other things were, the desiccated human forms wrapped in linen gauze, standing perfectly still but upright and seemingly animate.

"Are those...?" Jack began.

"Reanimated mummies," said Doc, shaking her head. What was the Silver Star's fascination with dredging up corpses to fight for them?

"Great," sighed Jack. "Well there's your strong magic. I count eight of them."

The haze seemed to part enough that they could see the central figure on the dais, dressed in flowing robes and wielding a sacrificial dagger like a conductor's baton.

"Surprise, surprise," he grunted. "Look who's throwing this party."

Doc squinted and caught herself before she could cry out. "Maria Blutig."

She spun to face the chained figure to her left, and Doc saw the man against the obelisk was Edward Willis. "Jack," she whispered. "It's Duke."

The smoky atmosphere began to swirl and move as the dais began to reverberate with the acolyte chants, vibrating and amplifying the tones. The room thrummed with the pulse of otherworldly sound, and for the first time Jack could see the other obelisk on the right. A blond woman was secured with metal chains, and her front looked as if it had recently been dyed dark red. She slumped against the chains, motionless.

"We've got to get to him," Doc urged. She took the lodestone from her neck and tucked it away in her satchel. It would only serve to give away their position.

"Working on it," Jack said, whipping one end of the climbing rope around the gallery column and catching it with his other hand. He began to tie a strong knot as Maria approached Duke. She gave a smile, flush with arcane power as the chants and amplified thrum continued.

"Even now that you have witnessed the deaths of your crew, Commander Willis, are you finally willing to serve the Astrum Argentum and its glorious master, the Great Beast of Mankind, Aleister Crowley?" She leaned in close and lifted his chin with the flat of her blade.

"Crowley is an abomination," Duke grunted. "And so are you."

"Atta boy, Duke," said Jack under his breath. He looked at Doc, who had un-holstered her revolver. "You and Deadeye cause a distraction. I'm gonna try to get to Duke."

Doc bit her lower lip as she watched him slip his foot into a loop at the end of the rope. "Aw, gee, here we go…"

"Well then, Commander. You have caused us serious harm, and your drive technology is now in our possession. Since you will not give yourself over to the service of our master, I no longer have any need of you. You will become the final blood sacrifice in the summoning of Ammit, Soul-Eater, Devourer of the Dead!"

Jack moved into position and readied a single .45. He'd considered one of the MP-18s, but it was a two-handed weapon, and he needed one hand to swing on the rope. Besides, if he went straight for a commando, he could disarm him and take his gun once on the temple floor. "Now!"

"Hey!" Doc shouted at the top of her lungs, popping up over the half-wall of the gallery. "She-Wolf of the Silver Star! Up here!"

Maria spun to see where the voice had originated, and found Doc standing defiantly on the upper level of the temple. "Ah," she replied. "I was hoping you'd make an appearance, *Doktor*." Without pause, she pointed in Doc's direction and barked an order to her commandos: "Shoot her."

The two soldiers nearest Maria took aim. Submachine guns roared and bullets flew. Doc clamped her eyes shut and instinctively flung her left arm in front of her. Spasms of iridescent light erupted around her as the bullets made contact, and were instantly absorbed by the shimmering bubble around her. She heard the soft metallic *tink tink tink* of pristine lead bullets falling harmlessly to her feet, but Doc was focused on the piercing look of surprise cutting through the haze from Maria. The She-Wolf of the Astrum Argentum was not used to having competition in the realm of occult power.

Doc stared at Maria, and Maria stared back. Deadeye glanced across the room at Jack, who nodded back at him, gripping the rope—and dove into the temple below.

- CHAPTER 19 -

Cipher banked the *Daedalus* away from the incoming fighter planes, taking a course due east. She throttled to full speed and continued to climb, listening for any radio chatter in her headset. Under no circumstances would she engage with Silver Star fighters while piloting solo. Without an expert tactician at the stick and gunners in both turrets, even a relatively small dirigible like the *Daedalus* was too large and slow a target.

As the airship topped 2,000 feet, Cipher caught a glimpse of the incoming squadron below her: eight biplanes, silhouetted dark against the desert floor. She was surprised to see them maintain their southwestern course, not deviating to engage her.

She wished desperately for the ability to see behind her, or to get a reading from the radio detector at the comm station, just to determine if she were being pursued, and by how many. If she switched the controls to the rudimentary autopilot system, she could get quick access to the detector, then be back in the pilot's chair when she knew more.

The fighter squadron would be directly below her in seconds. Her hand hovered over the *AUTOPILOT* switch.

Then, as she caught a glimpse of the circular RAF insignia on the lead plane, a burst of static came through the comms. "This is Royal Air Force Number 47 Squadron, calling unidentified airship on easterly heading, please identify."

Cipher felt the blood return to her face, and she cracked a surprised smile. She keyed the *TALK* button on the pilot's console. "This is the AEGIS airship *Daedalus* LR3-01, requesting assistance at Naqada. Pleased to make your acquaintance."

The voice in her headset was English Received Pronunciation, and gave Cipher a temporary feeling of familiarity and security, like a warm blanket.

"*Daedalus* LR3-01, we are at your service, with the regards of Sir Harold Marston. Lead on."

"Affirmative, RAF 47. Follow me."

Cipher banked hard and came around to a southeast heading, dropping down to an altitude of a thousand feet. She could see the planes of the 47th Squadron were Airco DH.9As, two-man light bombers with forward and rear-facing guns, laden with ordnance for dropping. Trailing the formation was a Vickers Type 56 Victoria, a round-nosed biplane freighter used by the British as a troop transport and flying ambulance.

"RAF 47, be advised I am sole crew aboard the *Daedalus*. Can fire forward mounted guns only."

"Affirmative, *Daedalus*. We've got you."

As she came in over the canyons northwest of Naqada, a small swarm of flies in the distance grew into sleek, black biplanes as they sped toward her to intercept. There were seven DH.9s and the Victoria to the Silver Star's six Fokkers, but something told Cipher that, even outnumbered and outgunned, these enemies were content to sacrifice themselves as a delay tactic.

"RAF 47, if you can engage those enemy Fokkers, I will lead the Victoria and one escort to the landing zone." Cipher's eyes squinted in determination as she gripped the controls, hands sweating on the throttle lever.

"Affirmative, *Daedalus*. Transport *Maxine* and escort *Tiger*, follow *Daedalus* to landing zone. Will cover your descent."

With the Vickers Victoria lined up to to port and the DH.9 on her starboard upper quarter, Cipher held the throttle at full speed and pushed forward on the stick, nosing the *Daedalus* toward the desert below as a dozen fighter planes clashed overhead.

☞

Jack leaped over the half-wall and swung down to the temple floor in a wide arc. His Colt spat fire and lead, and two cultists dropped to the ground, already starting to sizzle and smoke. Simultaneously, Deadeye cracked off shot after shot with the Winchester, dropping two commandos and a cultist, and putting a round into a mummy's head, which had no discernible effect.

Using the leverage of his left foot and the looped rope, Jack launched himself through the air, coming down on a mummy, which shattered to a pile of debris. He rolled out of the dive and came up facing a second desiccated corpse. Frayed, ancient bandages hung from its emaciated body as the undead creature moved slowly, slashing and growling as it stalked him. Jack opened with a left jab to the face, followed by a right hook, then a left hook. Nothing he did had any effect on the skeletal foot soldier. "These mummies don't go down easy!" he yelled to Doc in the gallery above.

Without warning, the temple was a sea of robes and daggers, the cultists stumbling over one another to get to Jack as he dealt with a more supernatural threat. Fortunately for Captain Stratosphere, a wall of shambling mummies surrounded him. Jack thought maybe he'd actually prefer dealing with the cultists instead.

Doc returned fire with her revolver, dropping a robed cultist. "Try to take their heads off! They may not be able to animate when separated from their seat of consciousness!"

Jack spun, backhanding the mummy in front of him. Its head cocked over to one side and rolled away to the corner of the room. Still it reached out with bony claws, grasping blindly. "Um, I don't think they *have* a seat of consciousness," Jack complained. "Now it's just a headless mummy...that *still* wants to kill me!"

Squatting into a wrestling posture, he came in low under the headless creature and grabbed it around the middle. It weighed almost nothing, and he easily juggled it into a throwing position. He launched the mummy with all of his might, and it sailed across the temple into two cultists, knocking them to the ground.

Jack felt a bony hand grip his shoulder and he spun to see the first mummy that he'd domed with a .45 slug. Reaching out with both hands, Jack tore one, then the other arm from their sockets, using the second arm as a baseball bat. He swung for the bleachers, taking the creature's head clean off and sending it across the room, where it hit one of the commandos in the face. In raising his hands instinctively to protect his head, the soldier dropped his MP-18 and fell back against the temple wall screaming in terror. Jack saw the mishap and closed the gap in seconds, as the throng of armed cultists pushed forward on him like a crimson wave.

"I'll take that," said Jack, kicking the trench sweeper into his grasp. He turned and saw a red wall of savage blades coming for him. Pulling the bolt back, he opened up into the wave of cultists, who stopped chanting and moved away to the center of the temple, cowering. Four more fell dead to the temple floor, and he led his aim up to the figure on the dais. "Back away from the obelisk, Maria!"

The remaining commandos raised their guns to fire, but two cracks from Deadeye's Winchester—each dropping a guard—got their attention. They stepped back, still clutching their weapons, but now pointed down. The handful of robed cultists still standing glommed together in a robed mass, tentatively awaiting further instruction from their leader.

The thrumming in the ground continued on its own. The energy beneath the temple had built to a critical level, an open clutch waiting to engage a gear.

There was a momentary pause, as Maria regarded the new arrival. Her eyes narrowed in hatred, and a modicum of fear, which she refused to acknowledge. "Captain Stratosphere! I was wondering where you were hiding. I've not had the pleasure since our encounter in the Himalayas." She licked some of the blood from the edge of her dagger. "You're looking well."

"Thanks, *Fraulein*," Jack sneered. "You're looking...evil."

Deadeye turned to look at Doc across the gallery and saw the gray-clad soldier appear behind her from the passage. "Doc!" he cried out. "Behind you!"

By instinct, she dropped her stance, lowering her center of gravity. Her elbow rocketed back into the soldier's gut, forcing the breath from him. Twisting to her right, she grabbed the soldier's submachine gun with both hands and dropped down, pulling both the gun and the soldier over the wall. The Silver Star commando fell headfirst to the temple floor, splitting his skull with a sharp *crack*.

Doc stood back up, holding the soldier's gun over the temple crowd. Deadeye flashed a thumbs up. Jack circled around the outer floor of the temple to gain a better vantage point, avoiding stepping directly onto the pulsing center.

Duke squinted through the roiling haze and made out the face of his former commander. "Good to see you, Captain," he puffed.

"You know I'm not one to miss a party, Duke," Jack quipped as he sidestepped around the remaining cultists toward the altar. "Especially when the guest of honor is a soul-eating demon, apparently." The sulfur-tinged smoke of dissolving bodies permeated the already-oppressive air as Jack leaped onto the dais, still brandishing the MP-18.

Maria inched back toward Duke, her sacrificial blade precariously close to his neck. "All I have to do is cut his throat, Captain! And his blood will call forth Ammit!"

Doc frowned. The MP-18 in her own hands was mostly for show. She knew from past experience how terribly clumsy she was with these things. "She's right, Jack! Don't let her get close!"

Jack, however, didn't have a problem with the weapon. He aimed the long-barreled submachine gun in Maria's direction. "Stand back, Maria!" he warned. "Your demon-summoning days are over!" He found Deadeye in the gallery and nodded at the obelisk.

Deadeye racked a round into the Winchester's chamber and took aim. The carbine cracked twice, and the chains slid down from Duke's body.

Duke saluted his erstwhile comrade, happy to be free once again. "Ah! Thanks, old boy!" In a tense ballet that seemed like forever, he edged slowly away from Maria and the obelisk, toward the altar, where Jack held the room at gunpoint.

Jack handed him the submachine gun. "Here, Duke. Take this pea shooter," he instructed, freeing his nickel-plated .45s from their holsters at his waist. "More comfy with the twin sisters anyway." Duke grabbed the MP-18 and brandished it without pause, keeping a watchful eye on the occupants of the underground chamber. Jack thumbed the hammers on both pistols simultaneously and addressed the agents and minions of the Silver Star. "Now all of you wizard wimps drop your weapons!"

Doc rolled her eyes. "Not with the wizard wimps again," she muttered.

A commando near the far exit under the gallery floor raised his submachine gun, ratcheting back the cocking bolt. Jack's Colt responded, and the soldier slumped to the ground.

"I said *drop. Your. Weapons.*"

The clatter of guns on the stone floor was followed by the remainder of the guards and cultists slumping to the ground, as if simultaneously tranquilized. Their bodies immediately began to smoke and sizzle, acrid tendrils of vapor wafting toward Maria. As they were no longer useful as soldiers, their lives were now forfeit.

"Come, my servants," she chanted hypnotically. "Feed my power."

Doc felt the blood drain from her face as she realized what Maria was doing. "Jack!" she warned, "Maria's drawing the life force from her followers!"

Deadeye, Duke, and Jack had all seen the phenomenon of Silver Star agents dissolving into nothing more than piles of ash and random bone fragments, and the theory had always been that their essence transferred to the psychic energy pool of Aleister Crowley himself. But in this case, it was clear that the agents present were surrendering their lives to add to Maria's already considerable occult might.

The floor continued to vibrate with the same low thrum, and Maria's eyes suddenly flashed aglow with a piercing amber light.

Jack hailed the far side of the gallery. "Deadeye, if you have a shot, take it!"

The Winchester barked in reply, and the bullet ricocheted away with a ripple of light, a foot from Maria's head.

Anger boiling over, Jack lined up with both pistols and began alternating shots. "Oh no, you don't get away that easy!"

Left. Right. Left. Right. The twin Colts cracked with fury. Jack edged ever closer as he emptied both clips at his target.

Maria stood in place, gazing out at them with glowing eyes. Bullet after bullet careened off in all directions with shimmers of light as if skipping a stone across a pool of water. A low chuckle rose in her throat, and she turned her head to peer at Jack with a look that chilled him to his core. "Your lovely bride isn't the only one who can deflect bullets," she hissed.

Jack dropped the Colts and leaped at Maria, right arm cocked back to strike, but her left hand flew out and caught his fist. Discharging a savage bolt of electricity down his arm and through his body, a burst of ozone and a flash of light rocketed Jack backwards to land on his tailbone, slumped against a pillar.

"Captain!" Duke cried, but Jack was already staggering to his feet. He seemed dazed, perhaps too much so to notice the smoldering burns on his right hand. His entire arm was charred black, and the rolled cuff of his stolen gray uniform shirt was shredded.

Doc saw his wounds and wanted desperately to climb down the rope to join him on the temple floor, but she knew he was better served by her staying watch in the gallery across from Deadeye.

"Damn you, Maria," Jack huffed as he achingly stood upright and planted his feet. This time, he refrained from approaching her, but was unhappy about the seeming stalemate. His knees ached with the pulsing vibration from the floor.

Maria paused thoughtfully, cocking her head as she took in the sight of him, the ruddy-faced man who had been a freckled youth with strawberry hair, the man's hair now a sun-kissed dishwater blond. She recalled her encounter with the young girl in Central Park and a smile crept across her face. "You know, your daughter looks much like you."

Jack froze. Doc's breath caught in her throat. Duke glanced back and forth between them, puzzled.

The hair on the back of Jack's neck bristled, and his face flushed red with anger. "What?"

Doc blinked in disbelief. "How is—?"

"Except she has your green eyes, of course," Maria finished, looking directly at Doc with a wink.

"*What?*" Jack repeated, furious, yet impotent to act.

"And now, Captain," Maria snarled, "I must bid you *adieu*."

In that moment, Jack's rational mind switched off and his primal aggression took over. He ran at Maria again, almost reaching the altar before the chamber erupted in blinding light. Jack threw his arm up to cover his eyes, skidding to a stop in the center of the dais. The vibration in the floor pulsed one last time, and suddenly all was quiet and still.

Duke blinked his eyes open and scanned the hazy interior. "She's gone!"

"What was that about Ellen?" Doc shivered, despite the heat and thick atmosphere.

Jack scowled, his eyes roaming the temple floor. "She's bluffing," he said, almost placating. He began to feel the sting of the burns on his hand.

Doc wasn't satisfied with the answer. "Jack?"

"We'll talk later."

"Darn right we will."

As Jack continued to survey the temple, he muttered to himself. "She better be bluffing."

- CHAPTER 20 -

Cipher throttled back as she made the first pass over the canyon wall. She banked the *Daedalus* and it rolled gently to starboard. She scoured the plateau for a landing area and was surprised to find only the *Percival* at its moorage. The *Osiris* had long departed, apparently followed by the *Luftpanzer II*.

The occasional small vehicle fire blazed in the afternoon sun, as the smoldering bodies of Silver Star agents littered the canyon floor.

The Vickers transport *Maxine* came in gently and dropped for a landing, the escort *Tiger* rejoining the dogfight above. The occasional tracer spat down from altitude, kicking rocks and sand into the air on impact.

Cipher spun the *Daedalus* and dropped to a landing adjacent to the *Percival*. British troops from the transport sprinted to take tether cables and assist in mooring the airship. She powered down the engines and unstrapped from the pilot's chair, anxious to get outside and find Rivets as soon as possible. Although the misadventure had been his idea alone, she nonetheless felt some small responsibility for leaving him to an uncertain fate.

As she disembarked through the starboard side gondola door, Cipher was pleased to see the stout form of Sir Harold Marston approaching from *Maxine*. He'd apparently hitched a ride with whatever military unit that was presently securing the canyon valley and entry to the sundered Golden City.

Cipher craned her neck and shaded her eyes as she scanned the sky above. There were only a few planes left in the fight: one of the Silver Star pilots had abandoned the scrap and taken off toward the southeast at top speed, pursued by two of the 47th. She knew they'd never catch the Silver Star plane, which was much faster than the larger, heavier RAF bombers, but they made a good show of strength. The other Fokker biplanes, and two of the British DH.9s, had been shot down over the desert or the river. The remaining craft circled the canyon and found safe landings on the canyon floor.

"I say, Lieutenant," Sir Harold hailed Cipher as he drew near. "What's the situation here?"

Cipher found herself suddenly weak-kneed and overwhelmed with the lack of immediate danger. "Commander Holloway," she gasped. "He dropped down to the *Percival* to try to get it flying."

"By himself?" Marston gaped. Drawing a Webley service revolver from his side holster, he gestured at the open gondola door of the *Percival*. "Let's go!"

As a dozen British soldiers took up defensive positions around the mouth of the canyon and under the shade of the two light reconnaissance airships, Cipher led Sir Harold aboard the *Percival*. There they found only an MP-18 that had been dropped near the pilot's chair on the bridge. Working their way back, they found a pile of dust under a gray uniform that had once been a Silver Star commando. It looked like the man had been dropped down the ladder from the top hatch. The crew quarters had been ransacked, but the engine room remained mostly undisturbed, save for a single DiMarco-Edison dynamo missing from the normal array of ten.

A horrible truth began to sink in upon Cipher. The Silver Star not only had possession of AEGIS perpetual motion technology, but the engineer most knowledgeable about it in the world, aside from the designers at Edison's lab in West Orange.

CB

Leaving Cipher to recover her wits in the shade of the airships' combined envelopes, Sir Harold led four soldiers armed with rifles into the sunken city, where they found Doc, Dead-eye, a wounded Jack, and a shell-shocked Duke in the great temple chamber, along with the empty vestments of eighteen Silver Star cultists and six commandos. Several linen-wrapped body parts were scattered through-out the large room, and four of the *Percival*'s crew lay dead in a pile in the southwest cor-ner, bled dry. The body of navigator Lucille Pimm hung limply from the chains around the obelisk opposite its empty, but equally bloody, twin.

It was sight unlike anything Sir Harold Marston had ever seen, despite a long and dis-tinguished adventuring and military service career.

With the soldiers' help, Jack and his crew were evacuated to the canyon above, while the fallen AEGIS specialists were loaded onto *Maxine* for return and burial.

The sun dropped lower in the western sky. Sir Harold held a sort of military court at the *Daedalus* moorage, taking reports from scouting parties who returned with news of a crashed plane or a smoldering uniform. AEGIS had mobilized a group of scientists and specialists out of Qena. They would be arriving within the hour. All of the crash sites had been checked out, and one British pilot had been recovered, in serious condition.

The reunion of crewmates was bittersweet. While they'd found Duke and the airship *Percival*, they'd lost Rivets and a piece of proprietary technology, and Duke had lost his entire crew. It was a decidedly mixed bag, and all things considered, a losing one.

Cipher returned from the *Daedalus* bridge to report her findings on the radio detector scan. "I managed to pick up a slight ping from the *Luftpanzer*, heading due south from here," she said. "The *Osiris* is long gone. It might as well have never been here."

"But it was," Deadeye noted.

Doc appeared preoccupied with their recent encounter with their seemingly unkillable arch nemesis. "Maria Blutig is using more complex magic than we've seen before."

"I still think it's illusion," Jack maintained, right hand throbbing under fresh bandages. "She didn't really teleport away—she just used a visual display to mask her exit. Same with the *Luftpanzer* disappearing over the Bahamas back in '25."

"Still a bloody impressive bit of illusion," Duke countered somberly. "And her hypnotic powers are not to be underestimated."

Sir Harold nodded in agreement. "Too true! So sorry, old boy."

"What happened?" Doc asked, smoothing back a lock of her old comrade's dark hair.

Duke sighed, wincing at the memories as they flooded back. "We engaged a squadron of Silver Star fighters over Lake Geneva, and took damage to the outer envelope and several ballonets. Rather than ascend, which would have been too risky with the leaking ballonets, we tried to hug the mountains as we entered the Italian Alps."

"Did you radio for help?" asked Jack.

"Of course. But there was too much interference from the mountains and the severe weather system the *Osiris* was riding for much signal to make it out. Before we could set the engine self-destruct and abandon ship, we'd been boarded. The commander of the *Osiris* is an Austrian fellow called Captain Hummel, but I heard him referred to by the crew as '*Schwarzhund*'. The Black Dog. They rafted the *Percival* to the *Osiris* and took us to rendezvous with the *Luftpanzer* in Italy, and we were transferred to Maria Blutig's oversight."

"That must have been terrible," Cipher frowned.

"It was far worse than I would have thought," Duke remembered. "They used strong arm techniques and threats of prolonged torture, but what Maria mostly focused on was a combination of drugs and hypnotic mysticism. She kept going on about making us change our allegiance, and when that was an obvious non-starter—bless my crew, every one of them—she started talking about going to a sunken temple of Set and doing something big, as a way to win back the favor of Aleister Crowley."

"Interesting," Jack pondered. "So her losses over the past two years have brought her down a few notches?"

"It appears so," said Duke. "Not that it's made her any less feared among the rank and file. Hummel even employed a faction of the Cult of Set in Cairo to interfere if you got too close. It really did appear that Maria and Captain Hummel were trying to get a win. And it would have been hard not to. They could take the *Percival* and reverse-engineer our most advanced AEGIS technology down to the struts, or they could try to entice one or more well-trained AEGIS field operatives to bring their knowledge and skill to the Silver Star, and if that didn't work, they could conjure an ancient demon to let loose in Northern Africa." Duke wiped a bead of sweat from his forehead with a bandanna. His lips were chapped from thirst and sun exposure, his face sunburned red. "Or they could have taken the man who knows almost everything about the current state of our weapons and technology, which is what happened."

"So what now, Duke?" asked Doc.

Jack shook his head, muttering under his breath. "Your whole crew..."

But Duke heard the comment, and was quick to defend himself. "Don't remind me, old man. I'll be reliving those horrid moments to the end of my days."

Jack nodded, wincing. "Do you think the Silver Star got much from the *Percival*?"

"Just one of the generators," Duke said. "They never really had time to do anything drastic, since Maria spent most of the journey here focused on getting me to change my allegiance."

Deadeye kicked his boot in the gold desert sand. "Edison's gonna pass a brick when he finds out."

Marston suddenly perked up. "I say, Willis. Why not take some of the lads in the 47th, and go retrieve the missing dynamo?"

"Do you mean it, Sir Harold?" Duke's eyes widened. "I'd love nothing better!"

Jack smiled. "Great idea, Duke." He considered the situation before them: one supercarrier, *Osiris*, had taken off relatively early to parts unknown. One aerocarrier, *Luftpanzer II*, was headed to the south. Either ship could be carrying the dynamo, Commander Carl Holloway, or both. The "good guys" were in possession of the *Daedalus*, down a broken dynamo and an engineer, and the *Percival*, minus a stolen dynamo and its entire crew.

And it sounded very much like Maria knew the intimate details of Ellen Starr's lineage.

None of these facts were ideal in Jack's mind, but neither were they insurmountable, as far as he was concerned.

In consultation with Sir Harold, it was decided to return to Cairo to repair the airships and recruit a new crew for the *Percival*. It would also be necessary to replace Rivets in the *Daedalus* engine room, even temporarily, so they hoped. They would need to wire their field reports to AEGIS headquarters and await subsequent orders, and Doc would obsess over sending telegram after telegram to New York, until her aunts replied to let her know Ellen was safe and sound.

There was only one mechanic even remotely qualified to join AEGIS as a ship's engineer

—a young Egyptian student at the University —and Duke lay claim to him first. Jack worried until Sir Harold checked with his contacts in the region and found mention of a talented mechanical whiz kid working for the RAF at the airfield in Mombasa. So Kenya would be an extra stop, albeit along their proposed route.

Asim Al-Hamal, the Egyptian soldier who had so expertly driven the Crossley truck during the chase by the Cultists of Set, had approached his commander in the Army for transfer to an AEGIS assignment, only to be screamed out of the CO's office. But within 24 hours and a flurry of paperwork from Sir Harold's field bureau, Asim was honorably discharged and commissioned to the *Daedalus* at the rank of Lieutenant. Jack was impressed with the young man and looked forward to training him as a backup pilot. He was already a fearless driver, and his marksmanship scores were decent for never having seen actual combat.

A general memo went out to all AEGIS field offices worldwide: the Silver Star had deployed what appeared to be the backbone of an impressive and dangerous aerofleet in the form of the two great airships, *Osiris* and *Luftpanzer II*. Any contact or sighting of either ship was to be reported to AEGIS Command immediately. The Daedalus-class airships *Cerberus*,

Achilles and *Vayu* were deployed into general service, and the AS4 series "service & transport" dirigibles *Galahad* and *Odysseus* were brought on-line.

And Thomas Edison offered a personal reward of $100,000.00 for the safe return of Commander Carl "Rivets" Holloway. Matching offers began to be added almost immediately, and by the time the sister ships *Daedalus* and *Percival* left Cairo, the reward had skyrocketed to two million American dollars.

- CHAPTER 21 -

Maria stalked into the radio room aboard the *Luftpanzer II*, surprising the Canadian comms officer at his station. He stared at her for a terrifying moment before she spoke.

"Give me the room," she ordered quietly.

"Yes, ma'am," the officer replied nervously, bolting for the door as fast as he dared.

Maria sat at the wireless, tapping out a message for The Master.

WOLF MOTHER TO A.A. CMD—

HAVE AEGIS DYNAMO & CMDR. CARL HOL-LOWAY OF DAEDALUS CREW & AEGIS AERO-NAUTICS DIV. AWAITING ORDERS.

She sat at the wireless radio for several minutes, playing various fantasy scenarios over in her mind. This excursion had been a triumph, despite the loss of their own soldiers and cultists. Human life was cheap. The Great War had proved that to the world. There were always disaffected, angry people, and such people were easily led down a dark path of scapegoating and lust for personal power. Maria was especially good at recruitment. She would have their ranks replenished in no time. Airplanes were easily procured with enough money, and the Silver Star's coffers were currently bursting.

She snapped back to the current moment as the first encoded beeps came across the receiver. This was direct from Astrum Argentum Command.

A.A. CMD TO WOLF MOTHER—

WELL DONE. PROCEED TO KO KHRAM SIAM NAVAL BASE FOR PROVISIONS. MASTER WILL CONTACT YOU PERSONALLY FOR MORE INFO.

Maria read the last part again: *Master will contact you personally...*

Rejoicing, the She-Wolf of the Astrum Argentum stood and tore the page with the received transmission and deciphered version from the radioman's notebook. Pocketing the slip of paper, she exited the radio room, anticipating a rare astral visit from The Master when she retired to her quarters later.

In the meantime, she headed to the bridge. Captain Ecke, and the *Osiris'* Captain Hummel, would be interested to know their new heading was across the Indian Ocean to Siam.

CR

As wary as Duke was about taking on a new crew, he couldn't complain when it came to the candidates. Each had undergone an exhaustive vetting and recruitment process through Sir Harold's field office, supervised by AEGIS Command.

The college boy, Darius Mahmoud, was an electrical engineering genius, halfway to a doctorate degree at the age of 26. The engine room on the *Percival* was a dream come true.

The new bridge crew consisted of navigator Lieutenant Ian Fraser, a handsome Scotsman formerly of the 47th Squadron; communications officer Lieutenant Peter Farmingham, a short, bespectacled Englishman formerly of the Royal Army Engineers; turret gunner Lieutenant Kate Shakespeare, an Englishwoman of 30 fresh from the AEGIS Academy in Cairo; and backup pilot/gunner Commander Sheila Barrett, an Australian pilot from a now-defunct ANZAC support squadron, who had flown the transport *Maxine* as an auxiliary of the 47th.

Two shakedown voyages in as many weeks had Duke just a tad nervous as the *Percival* lifted off from Almaza. But as bad as the nightmares would get, he would never let it be known the level of trauma he'd endured, watching his original crew slaughtered like sacrificial animals. If anything, he'd be more formal, keeping strict discipline and some emotional distance between himself and his subordinates.

But no matter what lay ahead for the *Percival* and her crew, Duke promised himself nothing like what had happened at Naqada— The Golden City—would ever happen to him again.

He wouldn't let it.

He'd die first.

☙

The *Daedalus* lifted off the tarmac at Almaza and climbed into the sunny blue sky over Cairo, and Jack McGraw leaned over the left side of the pilot's chair. "Bank a little more left," he instructed the young Egyptian at the stick.

Asim grinned, quite happy with his change in career.

Dorothy Starr stood next to Jack, leaning over the right side of the chair to look out through the window array. The morning sun bathed Cairo in warm yellow light, making it appear as a golden city in and of itself.

She squeezed Jack's arm and returned to her nav station. Jack followed, noticing Cipher's wry smile out of the corner of his eye.

"What's our course, Doc?" he asked, fishing a stick of Black Jack gum out of his chest pocket and folding it into his mouth.

Doc flattened the chart with a T-square and traced a line in red wax pencil down to the mid-coast of East Africa. "2500 miles to Mombasa," she said. "Bearing south-south-west."

Jack cast a glance back at his pilot. "You get that, Asim?"

"South-southwest, aye," Asim replied, watching the floating compass on the console as he adjusted the trim.

"*Percival* will rendezvous at the airfield there. At an average cruising speed of 90 miles per hour, we should arrive in just over 27 hours," Doc estimated.

Jack nodded. "Yeah, I don't want to push it without an engineer back there." He picked up the loose headset from Doc's console and held it to his cheek, keying the *TALK* button at the same time. "Deadeye, how's it looking topside?"

"A-okay, Cap'n," came Charlie's reply. "Skies are clear."

"Outstanding," said Jack. "Why don't you stand down and relax for a couple hours?"

"Affirmative. Thanks, Cap'n."

Jack put the headset down and noticed the melancholy look on Doc's face. "What is it?" he asked.

Doc sighed. "Just overwhelmed, I guess. With Rivets in danger, and new hands on the ship, and our arch-enemy knowing far too much about our daughter..."

For a moment, Jack eschewed protocol and wrapped Doc in a warm embrace. "It'll be okay," he promised. "When we're done with this mission, we'll take some time off and travel again, the whole family."

"I'd kind of rather stay home," she smiled sadly. "In Jersey, or California. Have a quiet summer."

Jack looked into her eyes and smiled. It was a look that said everything he needed to say. He leaned down and she met his lips in a soft, passionate kiss that tasted of licorice.

As he pulled away, Doc looked up at him and laughed. "Although you did promise me a trip to Paris."

"Whatever you want," Jack McGraw chuckled.

Dorothy Starr winked at him. "That's a dangerous philosophy," she said. "But I approve."

The End

ABOUT THE AUTHOR

Todd Downing's love affair with genre fiction dates back to his consumption of classic radio dramas and comic books as a child in the 1970s, which broadened into a general appreciation for scifi and fantasy media of all kinds.

He grew up in the greater San Francisco Bay Area, writing and drawing from a young age, his works ever-present in school literary journals and newspapers, and eventually on film. He married his high school sweetheart and moved to Seattle in 1991 where he began to write professionally, and worked as an artist in the videogame industry until his publishing company became a full time operation, while raising two children amid the chaos.

As the co-founder and creative director of Deep7 Press, Downing is the primary author and designer of over fifty roleplaying titles, including *Arrowflight*, *Grimmworld*, *Airship Daedalus*, and the official *Red Dwarf* RPG. He continues to write genre fiction for stage, film, comics, audio, and adventure gaming products.

Widowed to cancer in 2005, Downing remarried in 2009 and currently lives in a three-generation home in Port Orchard, Washington, with his wife, her mother, their daughter, four cats, and a flock of unruly chickens. Thankfully, he has an office with a door that closes.

Join the author's mailing list:
www.todddowning.com

Thrilling pulp adventure!
www.airshipdaedalus.com

Read the adventures of the Airship *Daedalus:*
A Shield Against the Darkness (Book #1)

*Assassins of the
Lost Kingdom* (Book #2, by E.J. Blaine)

The Golden City (Book #3)

Legend of the Savage Isle (Book #4)

The Arctic Menace (Book #5)

Plus:

AEGIS Tales
A Retro-Pulp Anthology, Volume 1

Primordial Soup Kitchen
A Collection of Short Strangeness

Calico Kids

The Parish

AVAILABLE NOW
in ebook and print!

www.ingramcontent.com/pod-product-compliance
Lightning Source LLC
Chambersburg PA
CBHW011209190726
48288CB00013B/3385